# CONSPIRACY
# OF LIGHT

## BY

## TERRY GOODMAN

COPYRIGHT 2002

WORLD THOUGHTS PUBLISHING, P.O. Box 3206 St. Augustine Florida, 32085-3206

WORLD THOUGHTS PUBLISHING is an Imprint of 1st WORLD LIBRARY.COM

Editors: Pam Youngquist, Cindee Delgado, Patti Summerville

Formatting: Cindee Delgado

Graphics: Public Domain /Author / Michael Crow, title page graphic

World Thoughts website: www.worldthoughts.com

FIRST EDITION

Library of Congress Cataloging-in-Publication Data

Goodman, Terry P.

Conspiracy of Light / Terry Goodman - 1st ed.

Includes Index.

ISBN 0-9711018-0-9

1. Metaphysics.  2. Physics-Philosophy.   3. Spirituality.   I. Title

To Pam, With all the Love in the Universe...

The Light is your protection,

The Darkness your teacher...

When you truly understand this you will realize that,

There is no darkness, and you need no protection...

# TABLE OF CONTENTS

ACKNOWLEDGMENTS .................................................................. VI
FOREWORD ............................................................................... VII
INTRODUCTION ......................................................................... XI
ACADEMY OF UR - GRADE 1: THE BASICS ..................... 1
    ONCE UPON A TIME ............................................................ 2
    THE GENERAL IDEA HERE... ............................................. 5
    DEVELOPMENT OF EGO ...................................................... 9
    UNITY: THE PRINCIPLE OF ONE ...................................... 11
    DESIRE ................................................................................. 13
ACADEMY OF UR - GRADE 2: THE PATH OF INVESTIGATION... 17
    THE MANY FOLD PATH ...................................................... 18
    COLOURS .............................................................................. 20
    NUMERICAL PATTERNS ...................................................... 26
    LIGHT .................................................................................... 32
    BACK TO THE EGO .............................................................. 45
    BROADCASTS AND THE BRAIN .......................................... 51
    FREQUENCY CHANGES ....................................................... 56
    MEDITATION ......................................................................... 58
ACADEMY OF UR - GRADE 3: APPLICATION OF ANCIENT
PHYSICS .................................................................................... 65
    PYRAMIDS, MERKABAH AND THE OCTAHEDRON .............. 66
    MORE NUMBERS AND OTHER STUFF ............................... 75
    SEVEN TO NINE .................................................................. 78
    GEOMETRIC INFORMATION ................................................ 85
    WHY AN OCTAHEDRON? .................................................... 89
    THE DIAMOND AND THE UNIFIED FIELD ........................... 94
    QUANTUM META-PHYSICS .................................................. 97
    THE MATTER OF MATTER ................................................. 102
ACADEMY OF UR - POST-GRADUATE: KINDERVERSITY ....... 105
    OBSERVATIONS .................................................................. 106
    RE-PROGRAMMING THE LOCAL CONTINUUM ................... 108
    THE UNIVERSE AS A FIELD OF CONSCIOUSNESS ........... 110
    THE LEGEND OF THE FALL THAT WASN'T ...................... 117
SUMMARY ................................................................................. 121
SUGGESTED READING AND OTHER SOURCES .................. 123
BIBLIOGRAPHY .......................................................................... 125

# Acknowledgments

S pecial thanks to the following, all of whom contributed, either knowingly or inadvertently, to the formation of this text.

Pam and Kristen Youngquist, Cindee and Black Hawk Delgado, Jim B. (who shall remain anonymous), Beth Bates, Gina Caruso and George Pappanastos, Rodney Charles, Toni Drew, Chelsea Flor, Steve Gaskin, Harmony, Jim Hurtak, John, Stanley A. Kilpatrick, Liz, Standing Elk, Path Finder, Jennifer Morton, Dr. Tony Minervino, Nanatasis, Silver Star, Patti Summerville, Tom & The Lady Jenna of the Antelope Retreat & Education Center, Tom Tilden (without whom I wouldn't be here to write this), Jim Little Trees, Lee Turner, Alan Watts, Willia, Shinzen Young, and Rosalyn Zephier... and the Aton Kabal...

Thank You All

# FOREWORD

## (Or Forewarned)

Coming from a Northeast Native American Woodland peoples, my elders and family taught me the traditional ways, but I also have a deeper understanding that extends to the Universal Messages. This has put me at odds with many people at times, especially "Traditionals." I am sometimes even at odds with myself. You see, I am a clan mother and a wisdom keeper, someone who must ensure that our Turtle Clan teachings and traditions will pass on to the next generation and be adhered to appropriately. I have found that if we use our traditions as guides for living in a good way with all our relatives, and if we truly believe our oral histories and prophecies passed on to us from our ancestors, we should easily be able to understand the Universal Messages. How can we not understand? The Original Instructions were given to all the peoples of this world and contain the same Universal Messages. Creator gave us our minds and Free Will in which to question all that is around us and to go beyond the limitations we impose upon ourselves out of fear and a need to control the uncontrollable... SPIRIT.

Sadly, we have somehow gone astray from these original Instructions.

I have listened to and learned from many wonderful elders. My greatest teacher was my clan mother, the late Grandmother Doris "Mourning Dove" Minckler. She taught me about unconditional love and demonstrated it in all her thoughts, words and actions, especially toward those who appeared unlovable. She understood and used not only our Abenaki traditions, but also the teachings of Christianity. As an amazing and true seer, she understood SPIRIT and the UNIVERSAL MESSAGES that Terry has also come to understand and now translates for us within the context of "Conspiracy of Light".

Meeting Terry was like a strong wind blowing the veil from my eyes, allowing me to see clearly the universal truths that I already knew. He is a mirror that shows me who I am and this allows me to laugh. Our friendship has blossomed since we first met through our dear friend Pam Youngquist. During any conversation with him, whenever I hesitate and search for the right words to express spiritual knowledge, Terry nonchalantly continues to explain the "indescribable" without missing a beat. This book and discussions with him have thrown open the doors of my mind, allowing me to forever expand into the vastness of the universe. Universal knowledge opens our minds to so many ideas that is it astounding. So who is Terry? A seer? A teacher? An intercessor? He is all of these and none of these. He is simply one of us.

We need to look deep enough into the pure meaning and basics of each spiritual tradition and religion. When we do, we will see that each claims that we all come from the same source, whether that source is called God, Great Spirit, Creator, or numerous other names. Each tradition or religion claims that we contain spirit, the same spirit of the original source. It does not take a genius to realize that if we all come from the same source and we are all part of the same source, then we are all One. Our difficulties and lessons come from attempting to live in right relationship with one another according to our Original Instructions, that simply put, are about unconditional love and unity.

It is my prayer and hope that you will find this book delightful, inspiring, and truthful. Terry has a trust and innocence of and for the Universal Knowledge that we all have access to, if we only let go of our fear and Ego. The simplicity with which Terry is able to connect some of the greatest religions and traditions together is not only enlightening, but also humorous. Let the words contained in this book free you of the limitations that you have accepted.

Then perhaps you will be able to laugh as Terry does... or any of the truly Wise Ones.

Nanatasis Bluto-Delvental
Turtle Clan, Western Abenaki
October 15, 2001

# Introduction

The information contained herein is an attempt to convey a level of understanding into language that essentially cannot be described by the use of that language. This leads us to the challenge of how to describe the indescribable. The solution is to do the best that I can, and hope it will be enough. The information presented here is for the most part, metaphorical in nature and is only the tip of a vast iceberg of such information. It is not intended to answer all your questions, but to point you in a direction where you can find those answers for yourself.

The majority of the information can best be described in traditional terms by the word prajña. Loosely translated this means "unqualified knowledge". The information stands on its own and seeks no outside validation. It is what it is, and the validation that comes, comes from within - a piece of the puzzle of which, everyone has and is a part. The idea is to put your own pieces of the puzzle together, and share it with others who care to do the same, so that we can all see how the pieces fit perfectly together to form the One Big Picture.

Much of the terminology being used may seem to be overtly intellectual. The reason for this is simple - this is the way it presented itself. While intellect is usually viewed as a function of the brain, the truth of the matter is that *the true seat of intelligence lies in the Heart*. It is the only center from which any truly intelligent interpretation or decision can be made...

# ACADEMY OF UR

# GRADE 1:

# The Basics

# Once Upon A Time...

In the Beginning (the point of time-space in which anything seems to begin) God reportedly created the Heaven & the Earth. This concept has been brought to our attention at this particular point of time-space, in an attempt to give us some insight regarding the Mystery of Creation and our part in it. Once again a turning point has been reached in the Evolution of what is referred to as "the human experience". A paradigm shift is occurring and the old limiting levels of conceptual reality are becoming unsustainable. In essence, we are standing on the threshold of another beginning.

What is being presented here are tools of consciousness designed to help expand the level of awareness, and give a greater understanding of who we truly are and why we are here. Actually the question is not so much, *why are we here*? But more to the point, ***what*** *are we here*? You may or may not realize it yet, but we are participating in an on going birthing process, the outcome of which will bring about an experience of total and unlimited Freedom. A Freedom far beyond the conceptual confines of our current agreed upon level of understanding. The key to that new level of understanding lies within experience. And the doorway to that experience lies in the Now. And that, as you will see, is where we must Begin...

The Point of Creation is the Now. What is meant by this, is that the creation of the universe is an on going process, it is not static or linear, although it can be experienced as such. Creation isn't something that happened a long time ago in some far off nebulous point of space, it's happening right here, right now. It's an ever expanding, continuous cycle, without end -- a sort of work in progress, and you are an integral aspect of the process. The simplest way to explain your role in this process is that you are a conscious focal point of a self aware universe, experiencing itself through you, as you. Knowing this as a concept is one thing, experiencing it in your every day life is quite another. It can be done, with practice and patience, once you know how.

The first thing you should know is that the active point of entry to working with this process is the Now. By the Now, we mean exactly where your body is, because your body is always in the Now. The Now, being the only truly active point along the time line and your tool of access is your attention. This basically means keeping your body and your attention together at the same place. The importance of this will hopefully become more apparent as we continue. Once you learn to be fully where you are, *always*, you will find that you are in a perfect position to understand what is occurring during this seeming time of accelerated growth and change.

Most of you are well aware of the fact that everything seems to be changing very rapidly. You are probably also aware that the way life, (human life) is being conducted here, cannot continue in the same fashion much longer. Well, you're right, it can't, for the simple reason that it's not supposed to! We are all rapidly coming to the end of our school year so to speak, and graduation day isn't that far off. Due to the interpretation of some ancient prophecies, many of you thought until quite recently, that we were living in the *End Times*.

The general, limited level of awareness that has developed here on Earth during this last cycle spawned the interpretation by some to mean doom for humankind, and worldwide devastation in the form of great Earth changes. Actually, the Earth is always in a constant state of change, and so are we. Truth be known, the only thing humankind is doomed to is Perfection, and the only devastation that may occur will be to the limited sense of self that many have been experiencing of late.

We have all been involved in a grand experiment, the scope and magnitude of which is far beyond the level of conceptual understanding. We have all been suffering from a strong dose of self-induced amnesia and are just starting to return from our self-imposed exile. In other words, we're finally starting to remember what's really going on here.

# The General Idea Here...

**E**ach time you come into this particular world through the process of birth, you come in with many divine qualities, two of which are complete trust, and a strong sense of Unity. This is because, in your deepest, most natural state, you are a unity being and trust is an integral part of your nature. When you are in this state, you understand that every form you see and everything you come into contact with is directly related to you. You instinctively feel the connection, much in the same way you feel the connection between your leg and your foot, or your fingers and hands. Trust is an attribute in this state of Divine awareness, rather than an issue. It simply would never occur to you not to trust another being, any more than it would occur to your leg not to trust your foot. Your natural state of conscious being is one of total harmony and freedom. You know who you are and what you are. You see and understand the constant interplay of life, light, energy, and conscious intelligence. You see and understand how all of these things are able to harmoniously combine and interact to form whatever experiential level of consciousness you choose to, or happen to be, participating in. Of course you love all of it - you feel totally at peace and are One with the whole thing. You're a part of it, and it's a part of you.

An interesting thing happens when you, or rather we, come in here. We retain these feelings, but not our memory. This seeming lack of memory is one of the main keys to understanding what we commonly refer to as The Earth Experience. So, let's explore this predicament we all seem to find ourselves in, which we will call **The Academy of Ur... ~ Or Planet Earth**.

On Earth, nature is one big harmonious interplay of energy, light, life, colour, and sound, much the same as it is throughout the Universe(s). And this is where it gets interesting. You see, there's this -otherwise - highly intelligent group of beings on Earth that for the most part, don't seem to be aware of this, let alone understand any of it. Not only that, two of them seem to be something called your parents, and they somehow have gotten steward-ship of you.

When you first arrive on Earth, you still feel deeply connected to everything; in fact you don't see any difference between yourself, your mother, the bed or the wall. As far as you're concerned, it's all you. And in point of fact, you're right, it is all you. But, for some reason, no one else seems to see it that way. It's somewhere about this point that something called confusion starts to set in.

Now, you would really like to set them straight about the whole affair. After all, you still feel directly connected to the source and you did just come from there - where ever that is - but for some reason you don't seem to be able to communicate with these beings. You also seem to be, somehow attached to a soft, sensitive, extremely uncoordinated vehicle (i.e. body) that you can't find the operating manual for.

## Welcome to the Experimental Zone, Entry Level 1; Planet Earth.

OK, you've been through this type of situation before, and you'll get through this one just as well. However, something seems a little different about this place though you can't quite put that thing called your finger on it right at the moment. (At this point, it's a major accomplishment if you can manage to get your finger into your mouth!) You knew what was different about this place before you got here, but now that you're here, you don't seem to be able to remember anything. And that is precisely the point of this particular adventure. It's the pivotal point, around which revolves the entire curriculum of the Academy of Ur (i.e. Earth School).

You see, one of the ways of looking at all of this is that Earth is sort of like your masters course, and your masters thesis is your life. The place that you are currently experiencing called planet Earth is in one of the many areas known as experimental zones. These zones are created and designed to provide an experiential level of consciousness within which, the development of the Nephesh - נפש or uneducated soul (ego) can take place.

This brings us to the reason why we don't seem to have any memory of what went on before we got here. The curriculum here, as it pertains in particular to Western thought, seems to be in the form of something very much like a giant *labyrinth* with many pathways that seem to lead nowhere. (If you switch the letter spacing to "no where", you'll have the key). The objective here is to learn your way out of this illusionary labyrinth, and share the information with anyone who is interested. Of course, for a labyrinth to be truly effective, you have to be lost in it, and having no immediate access to the record banks within your main memory core does tend to present you with the illusion of being somewhat lost. Now, couple this with the condition of being small, uncoordinated, and unable to communicate, and you'll have the perfect setting for the stage upon which your grand adventure can now take place. It's sort of like an elaborate game of cosmic *Hide and Seek*, only in this game; you're both hiding and seeking at the same time.

# Development of Ego

The stage has now been set for the development of the ego. The ego, in its most basic form, can be described as being a control mechanism that enables you to maintain a limited sense of self. The entire learning adventure here on Earth is based on having a limited sense of self. The ego manifests itself as being the resulting action produced by opposing dynamics. In this case, the opposing dynamics are (A) what you feel deeply within the core of your being to be true, and (B) what you're told is true when you get here.

The tension that is produced, because the two seem to be so diametrically opposed, builds to what might be called the breaking point. The release of tension that occurs from this break manifests in the form of an ego. The ego, in essence, becomes a sort of perceptual boundary line that forms between the essential self (or core being) and the intense onslaught of in coming negative information. (The word "negative" in this case should be understood to mean: negate-ive, as in to negate something, the action of which, is a form of limitation).

The ego's job now becomes one of being a kind of filter, through which, life's experiences are viewed. The active nature of the ego is one of comparison and separation, and its operational base line is the limited sense of self, or ego boundaries. Putting this as simply as possible, it goes something like this - we arrive here in what could be referred to as a fairly vulnerable state, we feel one way, we're told it's another - confusion sets in. We retreat to a seemingly neutral corner, we begin to construct a protective barrier, and from behind this we try to sort out what the heck's going on. This protective barrier is what eventually takes form as the ego. The emerging ego then attempts to create an over all view of reality based on the limited *in-coming* information as opposed to the *in-dwelling* feelings.

Because the ego's main function is to act as a protective barrier, the point of view experienced within the realm of the ego will always be one of separated observance and therefore limited. Now before we start getting any ideas that the ego is some sort of glitch in the cosmic program or maybe some type of horrible mind control device that's been implanted in our DNA eons ago by a race of highly advanced, though slightly warped E.T.s., we might want to think about this: The Essential Self or Ultimate Ground of Being - being all that is - wouldn't fully know it self because it has nothing to compare itself to. In other words, it has no point of reference. This being the case, the best thing it could do is to give itself an infinite number of different forms and then lose itself temporarily in those many forms - thus giving itself an infinite number of points of reference. This being lost in form (i.e. your form) is what gives rise to the ego and the ego is what helps give the Essential Self a temporary point of reference. Simple, right? In the Hindu/ Buddhist schools of thought this temporary point of reference is what is called Maya. Anyway, it's at this point that the main lesson plan starts to unfold.

# Unity: The Principle of One

An attempt will now be made to show how the core nature of the universal or *Essential Self* sets the guide lines along which, the lesson plan(s) are to unfold - the core nature being one of complete and total unity. The unity nature is the motivating force behind all forms of desire, earthy or otherwise. The unity nature and the ego work together to form the basic perceptual level of reality that determines the parameters of what is commonly called the $3^{rd}$ *Dimension*. The generally held view is that the $3^{rd}$ *Dimension* is an absolute, whose boundary lines are defined as being the realm of physical matter, or rather the world of form and substance. In truth the $3^{rd}$ *Dimension* is a perceptual point of view - not an absolute reality. However, it is this basic point of view that forms the ground or stage upon which, the drama of human life is played. It is the common ground, the constant line of the equation used to construct the program of *limitation*. The program of limitation can be likened to a computer program that operates from a small-restricted database. When the base line of any equation is formulated, whether in the field of theoretical mathematics or quantum physics, it is constructed on a theoretical supposition. If that theoretical supposition is based on limitation, the result of the equation will also carry a limited value. The way this translates into every day life is this - if your theory of life, (i.e. belief system) is based on a limited point of view, the resulting level of experience in that every day life will also be limited. Hence, you are operating in a life program that leans heavily toward limitation (i.e.: program of limitation).

This is essentially what many of us have been doing here. Basically speaking, the ego and the material based 3rd dimensional view of reality combine to form the basic structure of the aforementioned labyrinth. The Unity aspect of the *Essential Self* provides the motivational factor, in the form of seeking, because it perceives that it has lost its sense of unity and *desires* to regain it. This should basically give you a good understanding of the fact that everything we do is based on the *Essential Self's* desire for unity. The search for Love and acceptance in the everyday world, whether it be through our schools, our jobs, our relationships, our spiritual affiliations or what have you, is truly a quest for that sense of unity.

## Welcome to the Experimental Zone, Level 2 - Earth Sector; Academy of Ur.

# DESIRE

esire is the motivating force behind all levels of experience. It is what propels us from classroom to classroom, down the hallowed halls of the Academy of Ur - a/k/a Earth School.

Ur - אור also spelled Aur, is a Hebrew word meaning "Light".[1]

Desire has been the focal point of many spiritual discourses. One of the most memorable examples took place between the Buddha and one of his students. It seems the Master was one day approached by a student who wished to know how to obtain Enlightenment. The Master told the student that he must rid him self of all desire, the student thanked the Master and left. Some time later, the student returned to the Master and said, "I have done the best that I could to follow your instructions but I now find that I am desiring not to desire." To which the Master replied, "Now you're starting to understand."

What is being pointed out here is that desire is an integral part of the Essential Self. It is the driving force behind all conscious action. It is the active energy behind all forms of emotional expression. Desire is also one of the main components of the Essential Self that helps put the program of limitation into play.

A brief explanation of desire should give us a better understanding of why it works in the field of limitation.

One of desire's main objectives is to maintain a sense of unity.  This is quite easy to do, if not completely unnecessary, from the standpoint of the Essential Self since its perception of the Self is infinite and in no way limited.  Since little, if any, effort is required in this area, the main focus becomes the act of creation.  In other words, the desire to create new realms of conscious experience, such as this one in which it can learn about itself.  These new realms are very much like virtual reality games.  The more wrapped up in the game you get, the stronger the sense of the *reality* programmed into the game becomes.  This is exactly what desire enables you to do - get wrapped up in the game.  How this is able to occur is really quite interesting.  Simply put the lack of memory and the perceptual view of the ego together combine to form an illusion of separateness.  The Essential Self, now operating under the illusion of separateness, believes that unity has been lost and goes into search mode.  It then begins to assess all of the information available to it.

At this point, the information being received seems to come from two different sources.  One is the *still, small inner voice*.  The other being the much louder voice of what seems to be the outside world or world of consensual reality.  Since the one is so loud and bossy, and it does seem that you are in this seemingly outside world, the Essential Self (now experiencing itself as you), begins trying to reconstruct the seemingly lost sense of unity from the data available in that consensual world.  This data is not only limited in amount but is essentially *limiting* in nature.

Next, the aforementioned attribute of the Essential Self, called trust comes in to play.  You inherently *trust* that the information being handed to you (although at times, quite odd) is essentially correct. This, so to speak, is the point where you begin to get sucked into the game.

## Welcome to the Experimental Zone, Level 3 - Earth Sector: Academy of Ur.

After you've been here awhile, you are eventually brought around to the point where you start realizing that there's something more going on here than meets the eye ("I"). Some times this occurs through observing that, no matter how well you are able to attain the goals that society tells you are the basic keys to happiness - such as money, power, fame, success, sex, career, material possessions, etc. - you are still left feeling sort of empty and unfulfilled. Sometimes it happens because you have an experience that doesn't fit within the boundary lines of what is considered to be every day *normal* reality, such as a miraculous healing or a prophetic dream or vision. It could be a paranormal experience of some sort, a sighting, a close encounter, a near death experience, a past life memory, a sudden spiritual awakening or mystical experience. The list goes on and on. The point is that these experiences all shake the very foundation of what is believed to be normal. They have a tendency to make the day to day drama of every day life seem pale, if not a bit insignificant by comparison. You may have noticed that these types of occurrences are happening more frequently, to a greater number of people. What ever the type of experience may be, each one carries a significant message. The message being, quite simply that *"There are more things in heaven and earth Horatio, than are dreamt of in your philosophy."*

Until recently these types of experiences have generally been dealt with by viewing them either as momentary lapses of reason, or hallucinations of one sort or other, except by a very courageous few. A list of the names of these courageous few would include some of history's greatest spiritualists, scientists, philosophers and teachers. They have all, in one form or another made great sacrifices and reaped even greater rewards for their courage. They have pointed a way that, in the very least, is worthy of investigation. As the frequencies of these experiences quicken, and the amount of people having them becomes greater, the path of investigation begins to beckon to us, ever louder.

---

[1] Godwin's Cabalistic Encyclopedia, pg. 38, Llewellyn Publications, 1994

# ACADEMY OF UR

# GRADE 2:

# The Path of Investigation

# THE MANY FOLD PATH

The path of investigation is also the path of the Initiate. It is an ancient path that has been known throughout the ages by many different names. It is this path that the one called the Christ spoke of when he said *"Straight is the gate and narrow is the way and few of ye that will find it."* (Given the current interpretation of the Christ's message, it's a miracle if any of ye find it!) It is the path that is represented in the Arthurian legend that was followed by the Knights of the Round Table in their Quest for the Holy Grail. At various points it has been referred to as a road, a path, and a way. Eastern cultures have called it the *Tao* (way), the *Middle Road*, the *Eightfold Path*, and the *Fourth Path of Knowledge*. To some of the indigenous peoples of North America, it is known as *Canku Wakan*, (the Sacred Path). It is the combination of the many paths represented in the *Qaballah* that run between the 10 divine *Sephiroth* that composes the *Tree of Life*. Ancient Egyptian Initiates followed this path in the *Osirian Mystery School*. It is the *Rainbow* path, the path of the **7** stars, **7** stones, and/or **7** feathers of the Shaman.

This list could go on and on. Although, it is probably best represented in mythological terms as the ball of thread called a clew that was given to Theseus by Ariadne, so that he might find his way out of the Labyrinth after his battle with the Minotaur. (Clew, being the bases for the more current spelling and meaning of the word "clue".) It is this *Ariadne's Thread* that forms the unbreakable, indestructible link between the Essential Self and the limited sense of self that has been the general level of experience within this last cycle. It is also a sort of fail-safe mechanism that has been built into the program of limitation. Lack of awareness or outright denial of the existence of this Divine link has no baring on the link itself, only on its usefulness as a tool of liberation.

Since you are currently reading this material, it can be somewhat safely assumed that you have already begun your journey along the path of investigation. And although the path is circular and essentially leads to where you are now, it is one that once started, we find we must follow to its inevitable conclusion. This being the case, the Shaman's path of the 7 stones will be used to explain some of the steps that will be taken along the journey.

First, you should know that everything needed to undertake this journey already exists inside of you, and that this path should, by no means, be viewed as being the one and only *true path*. All paths are divine and should be honored. (Though admittedly, some are more direct than others.)

I have chosen to use this path because it serves up a broad base upon which many analogies relating to other paths can be drawn. Each of the 7 (stones, stars, feathers etc.) has its own particular colour frequency, which represents one or more of the essential divine attributes of the unified being. The number seven is itself a very sacred number that can be found in use throughout most spiritual schools. (7 seals, 7 chakras, 7 Heavens etc.) It also has a much deeper significance that will be explored further on.

# COLOURS

ou may find that the following list of colours, and their attributes will sometimes vary according to the specific teaching of any given spiritual school (i.e.: White, violet, and indigo are sometimes found replacing each other in certain instances). For the most part, they are all pretty much the same - at first anyway. It is suggested that you use whatever colour sequence feels the best or makes the most sense to you. Remember that *there is no one right way of doing any of this!* The right way will be the one that works the best for you. Also, it should be kept in mind that what works best for one, may not be the best, or in fact, work at all for another. The reason for this should become abundantly clear as we continue.

What follows is a list of the 7 basic colours of the *Inner Light Spectrum* along with their representative attributes:

1. **Red** ............. Courage, Confidence

2. **Orange** ......... Balance

3. **Yellow** .......... Creativity

4. **Green** .......... Growth

5. **Blue** ............. Truth

6. **Purple** .......... Wisdom

7. **Violet** ........... Change, Transformation

These are the primary colours in their most basic forms. Together they form a part of one of the keys, which will eventually enable you to de-structure the current program of limitation.

**Red**, the stone of **Courage** and **Confidence**, is the foundation stone from which all further steps along the path of the **7** stones are taken. It calls for the development and use of courage, which requires confidence; the courage to go beyond what you have been told, and investigate things for yourself. The courage to trust and listen to the *still, small inner voice*. The courage to face and go beyond fear. And, to have the courage to trust yourself, and most importantly, to find out who that *Self* is, and allow your self to be it.

Next is the **Orange** stone, the stone of **Balance**. In the dictionary, one of the descriptions of "balance" is given thus: "Mental steadiness or emotional stability; habit of calm behavior, judgment, etc." [2] The key here is *calm behavior*. Basically speaking, anything presenting itself to one that is operating from a state of calm centeredness (i.e. Balance) will be perceived with a greater amount of clarity. The word "balanced" carries the following definition[2]: "being in a state of harmonious or proper arrangement or adjustment".

Next is the **Yellow** stone of **Creativity**. It calls for the cultivation of your creative powers. The purpose of this stone is the mindful directing of energy. The reason for this is fairly simple - undirected energy tends toward chaos, and mindlessly directed energy tends toward destruction, while the mindful direction of energy (i.e.; creativity) tends toward harmony. The mindful direction of energy also helps by strengthening the already unbreakable *Ariadne's Thread* that connects the limited sense of self with

CONSPIRACY OF LIGHT

the Essential Self, whose main purpose and desire is
*CREATIVITY.*

Next comes the **Green** stone of **Growth**. Once
again the dictionary shows itself to hold a wealth of
information. The base word, "grow" carries these
meanings: "to increase by natural development; to
come to be, or become by degrees". The word
"growth" has this meaning: "development from
another but related form or stage."[2] Part of the key
here lies in the understanding that everything is
*related.* The purpose of this stone is to point out that
growth is a natural process of the universe, as you
also are a natural process of that same universe. We
know that in nature anything that stops growing dies,
and becomes recycled. So basically, if you wish to
continue your journey of mindful discovery, you
should probably continue to allow yourself to grow
and expand. You know the old saying, "Go with the
flow", or as the ancient Chinese called it, the Tao.

The next stop on the journey is the **Blue** stone of
**Truth**. The Blue stone is a little tougher to explain
because basically, most of the beings here that think
of themselves as being Human don't really
understand what truth is. This does not mean that
they're liars - it just means that they have only been
taught a *relative* form of truth. The truth isn't
something that you find outside of yourself. It isn't a
concept or something that comes into being simply
because you get enough people to agree upon a
particular point of view. Truth is inside of you. Truth
is a language. It is the language spoken by the *still,
small inner voice.* It is the language of the Heart, and
the place where you live when you speak from the
Heart. That place is called your *Circle of Truth.*
When you speak from that place, you are that truth.
This is the message of the Blue Stone.

The **Purple** stone of **Wisdom** is a little different, as it is more of a gift than a step. It is a gift that is given to you by all the other stones once you have thoroughly and patiently worked with each and every one of them. It is the mindful application of all the lessons taught by the other stones. Wisdom is insight, discernment, and understanding. Wisdom is measured by what you do with what you have learned. It is the use of the *Knowledge of Truth.*

The **Violet** stone is the stone of **Change** and **Transformation**. Change is the Universal Constant because the nature of the universe is one of constant change. In other words, the universe is continually moving, therefore it is also constantly changing. Since you are an integral process of the universe, it stands to reason that you also are continually in a state of change. This is a basic fundamental of life. Change is a process of Growth and Growth is the active principle of development. The progressive development of conscious awareness brings about a Transformation, and that Transformation takes place through the full assimilation and integration of all the lessons learned along the path of the 7 stones. It is the transformation from Initiate to Adept, from Seeker to Knower. It is the true meaning that stands behind the Biblical story of the *Virgin Birth*. It is the birth of the fully integrated Physical / Spiritual Being from this purely physical animal body. This transformation in turn brings on further cycles of change, growth, and development. It never really ceases, although there are periods of rest.

As was mentioned before, this is the colour structure in its most basic form, and this is by no means the end of the journey. There is no such thing. The word end should be read as meaning: a *point of transition*. Just as the level of awareness and understanding has become expanded, so too has the potential use of colours as tools. They can be used in many forms, for just about any task. Colour can be used for grounding, healing, clearing, and the further expansion of consciousness. It can be used in the form of directed or transmitted *Light* energy through a process involving visualization and directed concentration. It is an extremely effective tool of Liberation.

Colour and Music are very similar in structure, and as you will soon see, are intimately tied together (this goes for everything else in the universe as well). Just as each note has its own particular frequency, each colour occupies a certain frequency level within the Light spectrum. When certain notes are played in unison they combine to form a resonant harmonic structure called a chord. The same type of event also occurs in the colour spectrum. For instance, when red and blue are combined in equal amounts, they form purple. A lesser amount of red combined with blue produce a violet. These are harmonics of Light. The secret to understanding the higher vibrational levels of consciousness lies within the understanding of the *periodicity* of Harmonics, Sonic Structure, and Light, none of which can be separated from each other.

Just as learning to play music takes practice, learning to use colour effectively may also require a certain amount of practice. The best way to go about it is to start experimenting. Visualization is probably one of the more direct and effective methods of utilizing colour, although the use of coloured stones and/or crystals and actual light rays is also quite effective. Colour Therapy for instance is a form of phototherapy that uses colour to influence health, and also to treat various physical and mental dis-eases. It can be administered through the use of coloured light rays in the visible as well as the invisible spectrums. It can also be applied mentally through suggestion. In certain cases it has been found to be quite useful in treating conditions such as asthma, allergies, headache, kidney, and liver problems etc.

---

[2] Webster's Unabridged College Dictionary, 1984

# NUMERICAL PATTERNS

As you continue the investigation, you will find that there is an amazing treasury of information hidden within the numerological body of many ancient mystical and spiritual teachings. Within, the more esoteric forms of Hebrew mysticism, this type of study has been honed to a fine art (i.e. Merkabah, Zohar, and Qaballah). In Hebrew, this body of information is called *gematria*, a word that corresponds to the Greek word *geometria*, which itself pertains to the body of information contained in what is nowadays called *Sacred Geometry*. Sacred Geometry being one of the lines of information expounded in the Pythagorean school of thought. In truth all geometry is sacred, but then again, so is everything else (smile ☺).

Originally, numbers had a much deeper significance than is generally known of today. The early teachers of numbers viewed them as a sacred, spiritual, scientific language that they used to measure and explain how all energy flows in certain patterns, and how these patterns merge together to form everything in the Universe. This information was handed down through the ages from before recorded history, and points to being of Antediluvian origin as far as the linear time line is concerned. It was passed down to the lands that are now called Egypt, Persia, and India (as well as many others) and eventually to ancient Greece. It was in Greece that Pythagoras formed the information into a body of knowledge that was composed of 5 interrelated subjects. These subjects are: 1) Arithmetic, 2) Plane

Geometry, 3) Stereometry (solid geometry), 4) Astronomy, and 5) Music.

These were not taught as 5 separate courses. They were taught as 1 course that had 5 progressive stages or steps, each one leading to the next. It was presented in this fashion because he had a deep understanding that the nature of the Universe itself was one of constant or progressive unfoldment, and therefore he felt that the lessons should be presented in the same manner. These 5 steps contain most of what is known today as the teachings of Pythagoras. The intended purpose of this information was to show how the Universe operated, and how it came into being.

Pythagoras taught arithmetic first. According to him, if you didn't understand the spiritual significance of numbers, you wouldn't be able to truly understand anything else. This becomes much clearer when you see how the Pythagoreans explain the significance of the number **1**.

They called the number 1 Unity, which represented the nature of God. God or Unity being the essence of everything, seen and unseen:

"Unity is the principle of all things and the most dominant of all that is; all things emanate from it and it emanates from nothing. It is indivisible and it is everything in power. It is immutable and never departs from its own nature through multiplication (1 x 1 = 1). All that is intelligible and cannot be engendered exists in it: the nature of ideas, God himself, the soul, the beautiful and the good, and every intelligible essence. Such as beauty itself, justice itself, equality itself, for we conceive of each of these things as being One and as existing in itself.[3]

This is the premise upon which all-subsequent lessons, and levels of understanding were based. This is the original and true meaning of the number "1". Every subsequent number was understood to be an unfoldment of the Unity or number "1", not a division of it. (Pretty cool, huh? Guess they forgot to mention that in math class!) Qabalistic Hebrew terms refer to the number "1" as (*Aleph*), which represents the *unthinkable life-death, abstract principle of all that is and is not.*

Each number from 1 to 10 represents a sequential, developmental stage related to how Life and the Universe came into being. The actual starting point of the sequence begins with **0**, though at this point it is not actually viewed as being a number. The "0" here represents the eternal, the never-ending line, and is probably best described like this: *The Nature of God is a circle of which the center is everywhere and the circumference is nowhere.* In this sequence it represents the great stillness that lies at the center of all. It is the all-encompassing, non-moving state of absolute Be-*ness* that is imperceivable; therefore it is called non-being. It is the Great Nothing, called Ain אין by the Hebrews. It is the Sanskrit *Shunyata*, the Fullness of the Void.

The numbers map the progression of the Eternal Energy from the state of non-moving *Be-ness*, into the moving and more active states, or stages of Being. The state of *Be-ness* can be likened to the

*Deep, Dreamless Sleep of God.* The numbers illustrate how God wakes up everyday - each day and night being an eternity, or *Kalpa* (world cycle) as the Hindus call it. These progressive stages of unfoldment are mentioned in most spiritual teachings, though some are more poetic and veiled than others are. This is what is alluded to in the biblical story of Genesis.

The story of Genesis seems so veiled because the real significance of the story is not so much in the story itself, but in the numerical values and placement of the original Hebrew letters themselves within the structure of the text. When we look at the text of Genesis in its original Hebrew form, one of the first things that we notice is that there are no spaces between words, and no punctuation of any kind. What we actually see is a long series of figures all strung together. Each Hebrew letter not only had a numerical value that had a spiritual significance which related to a specific energetic component of the cosmos, but the letter itself was actually the symbol for that number.

The ancient Hebrews didn't use a second set of symbols to represent numerical values as is done today. The letter was the number and the number was the letter. In other words, hidden in what we have been told is a story of words, is another story that presents itself in numerical form. (This may help to explain some of the confusion surrounding this text.) The 1$^{st}$ five chapters of Genesis may quite possibly be part or all of the lost Tablets of Destiny that have been spoken of in some of the ancient texts, though for the most part there are very few who know what they're looking at or how to read them. One of the few exceptions is Stan Tenen's work on the subject that is being done at the Meru Foundation. (See references).

It's quite likely that the early Qabalists and some of the very early Christians knew about this. But for some reason the founders of the modern church that was started in Rome, either were not told of this, (???) or they simply chose to ignore it for reasons of their own.[4]

Okay, the next number is **2**. Pythagoras viewed it as the first increase; the doubling of Unity. This is where the barely perceptible motion of the "1" awakens and becomes the much more active "2" in the form of the Cosmic Mother and Father. These two are the active principles that stand behind the polar aspects of Yin and Yang, Light and Darkness, Positive and Negative (in their energetic form), and Male and Female. The number 2 is called *Beth* or *Bayt* in the Hebrew system, which is *the physical energetic support without which, nothing is.*

The interaction of these 2 brings about the 3rd or the number **3** in a very unique manner. What takes place here has to do with the principle of energetic dynamics. Carl Jung explains it like this:

> "Every tension of opposites culminates in a release, out of which comes the 3rd. In the 3rd, the tension is resolved and lost unity is restored."[5]

It was for this very reason that Pythagoras didn't pay too much attention to the number 2, because from his point of view it became the number 3 almost immediately. The number 3, which in Hebrew is called *Ghimel*, represents this same organic motion. Now this 3rd is the 1st born, whose name is *Light*. The Greeks viewed the number 3 as the first whole number because the tension of the 2 becomes resolved through the unifying action of the $3^{rd}$, or number 3.

Dr. Hans Jenny speaks of the Basic Triadic Phenomenon as inherent to the nature of the universe. Here the creative process is viewed as consisting of three interrelated fields:

> "The three fields - the periodic and the two poles of figure & dynamics - invariably appear as one. They are inconceivable without each other. It is quite out of the question to take away the one or the other; nothing can be abstracted without the whole ceasing to exist. We cannot therefore number them 1, 2, 3 but can only say that they are threefold in appearance and yet unitary; that they appear as one, and yet are threefold."[6]

This is what lies behind the biblical representation of the Holy Trinity. In geometrical terms, the number 3 is a triangle.

Interestingly, one of the things that seems to have been completely overlooked, if not entirely omitted from the later versions of the Bible, is that the Mother and Father of Light are Darkness. To understand this, we have to first look at what Light is.

---

[3] *Theon of Smyrna*, Wizards Bookshelf, Publisher

[4] *The Women's Encyclopedia of Myths and Secrets*, Castle Books edition, by Barbara G. Walker has some really good information on the subject.

[5] C.G. Jung, Psychology and Religion: West and East, CW II, 1953-78

[6] *Klymatik by* Hans Jenny, Basilius Presse Basel

# LIGHT

To begin with, we don't really see actual light itself. What we do see is a very few wavelengths of radiation that fall within a very narrow frequency range in the electromagnetic spectrum, that are being bounced or rather, reflected off of material objects (see spectrum chart, circled area). In other words, if you don't have material, you don't have perceivable light. From this standpoint, it becomes quite easy to understand how "absolute light" is "absolute darkness" in the absence of a material world. To take this a step further, we have to understand that the angular momentum of the sub-particles in the atomic structure is what gives substance to physical matter. No movement = no matter, no matter = no light. (See graphic page 34.)

Now following the progression from **0** to **3**, it goes something like this: "0" is the all encompassing everything in a state of non-motion. Everything being the raw substance of matter, i.e. atomic structure in a completely motionless state, and absolute light, which at this point is absolute darkness. This is the biblical *darkness on the face of the deep*. The first movement takes place on the sub-atomic level because the first energetic substance that goes into motion is much finer than the atomic structure itself. The Tibetans call this substance *Phowa* or Divine Thought. It is the reawakening Universal, Cosmic Consciousness.

Through a process we will call Super-Luminal transmission, the Phowa (Divine Thought), projects itself out and vibrates, or rather rings the dormant, raw substance of the Universe into action. This vibration or if you prefer, ringing, is the true meaning behind the biblical phrase, *and God said...* It is the *Word of God*, the Music of the Spheres, the very essence of the Universe and life itself...

This action gives substance to matter, and matter then reflects the ever-present radiation of absolute Light into a perceivable frequency range. To put it simply: the movement of the **1** activates the substance of the **2**, which gives birth to the **3** in the form of Light. (It's really very simple, once you get the hang of it.)

**Remember, only Light can create shadows...**

Now we come to the number **4**. Four is the active nature of the *Trinitized Unity* or number 3. It is the *Word* made manifest - the raw substance in action. This raw substance is represented as having 4 attributes, Earth, Air, Fire, and Water. The Hebrews viewed the number 4 Dallet, as: The *physical existence as response to life and all that, which in nature is organically active.* Pythagoras viewed the number 4 as being the image of the solid. It is the first square number.

Square numbers are any number times itself that results in a larger number than the one you began with, i.e. 2x2=4, 3x3=9, and so on. The only number this doesn't apply to is 1, (1x1=1). The plane geometrical form of the number 4 is the Square. The solid geometrical form is the tetrahedron, which is the first solid.

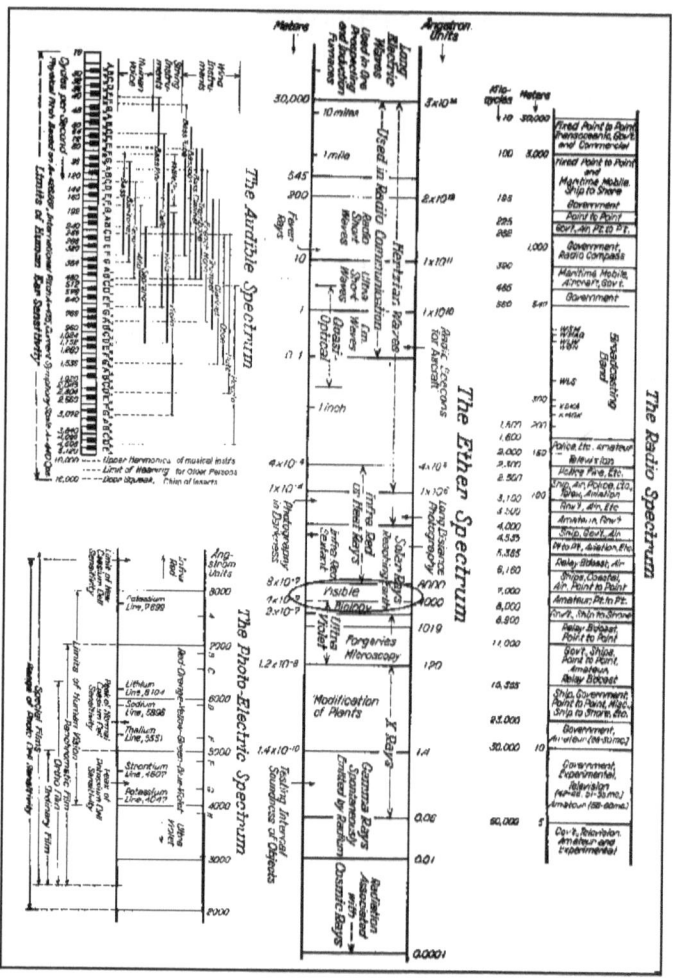

The Pythagoreans sometimes referred to the number four by two different names. It was either called the **Quaternary** or the **Tetraktys** depending upon its application.

The word Tetraktys refers to the many aspects of the Quaternary as a whole. It signifies the divine 4 in the field of Unity. It was sometimes symbolized by the triangle placed inside of the circle, the same symbol that is today, used by Alcoholics Anonymous. This is what is referred to as the *Squared Circle*, the triangle supplying "3" of the sides, the circle supplying the 4th. It was also symbolized by 10 dots in the form of a triangle. There is also a Qabalistic version of this called the **Tetragrammaton** where the dots are replaced by arranging the 4 Hebrew letters יהוה in the form of the *Tetraktys*. The word Quaternary usually refers to specific aspects regarding the number 4, of which there are at least eleven according to Pythagoras.

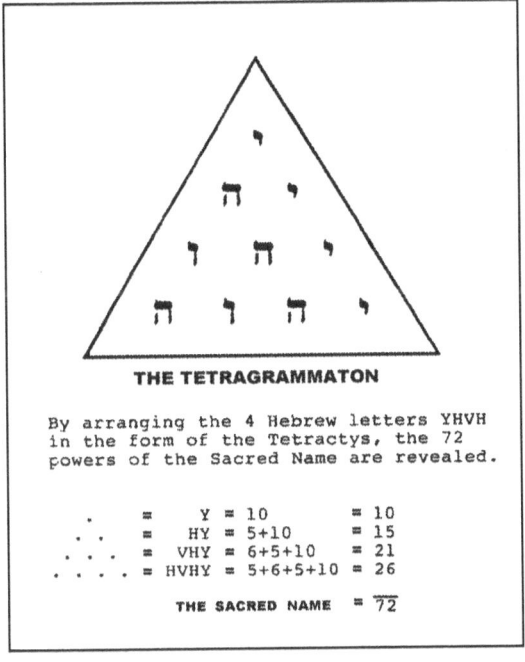

**THE TETRAGRAMMATON**

By arranging the 4 Hebrew letters YHVH in the form of the Tetractys, the 72 powers of the Sacred Name are revealed.

```
    .       =        Y   = 10         = 10
  .   .     =       HY   = 5+10       = 15
 .   .   .  =      VHY   = 6+5+10     = 21
.  .  .  .  =     HVHY   = 5+6+5+10   = 26
```

            **THE SACRED NAME**  = 7̄2̄

Now, it should be pointed out that the Pythagoreans not only placed great significance on each number itself. They also placed a very strong emphasis on the patterns that were formed by the way the numbers related to each other in a given sequence.

This pattern is called a Ratio. This was done because they understood that the Universe itself was made up of a multitude of interlocking, interrelated patterns, and by working with ratios it helped them to see and understand how all things are related. *(Ratio = Relationship)* It was one of the tools they used to teach the student how to recognize and read those natural patterns.

The first two of the eleven quaternaries are of numbers, one of which is made by addition, the other by multiplication. These quaternaries encompass the musical, geometric, and mathematical ratios of which the Harmony of the Universe is composed.

The 3$^{rd}$ quaternary states that the ratios found in the first two quaternaries are the same ratios found in all the lines, both straight and curved, that make up all geometric forms both plane and solid.

The 4$^{th}$ quaternary is that of the 4 Elements. They are presented according to their fineness or density. Number 1 is Fire, number 2 is Air, number 3 is Water, and number 4 is Earth.

The 5$^{th}$ quaternary is that of the shapes of the Elements. The Pyramid is Fire, the Octahedron is Air, the Icosahedron is Water, and the Cube is Earth.

The 6$^{th}$ is that of created things. The seed is unity (number 1), a growth in length is 2, a growth in width is 3, and a growth in thickness completes the solid and is number 4.

The 7$^{th}$ is that of societies. Man is the unity, and the family is number 2. The village is number 3, and the city is number 4. These are the elements of a nation.

The 8$^{th}$ are the faculties of judgment. Thought is the unity because it is the essence of unity. Science is number 2 because it is the science of all things. Opinion is number 3 because it is something between science and ignorance, and feeling is number 4, the sense of touch being common to all and all the senses are activated through contact.

The 9$^{th}$ is that which composes the living things, body and soul, the soul having three parts, the rational, the emotional, and the willful; the fourth part is the body in which the soul resides.

The 10$^{th}$ is the seasons of the year, through which all things take birth. That is spring, summer, autumn, and winter.

The 11$^{th}$ is that of the ages; childhood, adolescence, maturity, and old age. The perfect world which results from these quaternaries is geometrically, harmonically, and mathematically arranged... it is perfect because everything is part of it and it is itself a part of nothing else.

There are also many other quaternaries that weren't mentioned, one of which plays a very important role in the ceremonies of the indigenous peoples of North America. These are the four lateral directions, north, south, east, and west. There is also one that they may not have been aware of, the four atomic elements that form the basis of all life; they are carbon, oxygen, nitrogen, and hydrogen.

The next number we come to may at first seem to be out of sequence, but in point of fact, it makes perfect sense. That number is **10**. The Pythagorean name for 10 is *Decad*, from which we get the word decade, and it is a perfect number. The *Decad* is perfect because it symbolizes all that exists. In the Hebrew system the number 10, *Yod*, is the projection of the Unity (1 = *Aleph*) into the temporal continuity of the manifest world. The way we arrive at the Decad or number 10 is very simple: I+2+3+4 = 10.

You will realize that the nature of the universe, and all of life for that matter, is cyclic or periodic as well as rhythmic. Just as there is daily activity followed by nightly sleep, so too the universe is always quite active before each period of rest. This, once again, is where much of the confusion seems to lie regarding the story of Genesis. This is due in part to the habitual way that humans have of always viewing things in terms of the finite, and partly because Genesis was written as a story within a story. It might be more helpful if you understand that the word "*Beginning.*" In the biblical phrase that starts with "In the *Beginning...*" it is actually referring to the beginning of "motion" from the pre-matter state of non-motion, i.e. - the rest period.

The number 10 is also the basis for the Qabalistic *Tree of Life.* It is represented in the form of the *10 Divine Sephiroth*, or spheres that compose the *Tree* itself. There is an incredible amount of very beautiful and useful information contained in the body of knowledge known as the *Qaballah.* Though it can oft times be found to be a bit confusing, owing to the poetically veiled and sometimes secretive manner in which the information seems to present itself. Especially when what is actually a numerical code in some cases is read instead as grammatical language.

This type of interpretation may be the possible reason for the various dogmatic points of view that some of the differing groups studying the information seemed to have adopted. It basically amounts to something that could be called spiritual/political infighting and is probably not very useful. Unless of course the objective is in maintaining a status of "I'm right and you're wrong". In that case, it's highly useful. This is not meant to be a judgment, it is only an observation that might be of some help if and/or when you decide to delve into the matter further. All observations are open to constant revision. The most effective method of reading or studying anything is with an open heart and an open mind. This applies particularly well to the Qaballah.

Now comes the number **5**. Five is the number of the body of physical man, sometimes referred to as the *Robe of the Soul.* (The word *man* should always be read to mean mankind, <u>both female & male</u>.) The pentagon and the pentagram or the five-pointed star, which looks like an upright human form with outstretched limbs, symbolizes it. The 5 is most directly represented in the form of the five senses: sight, smell, touch, taste, and hearing; and the five fingers of the hand, and the five toes of the foot. The five senses are all processed and interpreted by the head, which is the director of all physical motion. Looking at the form of the pentagram, the head is represented by the uppermost of the 5 apexes and is the number 1, or Unity, among the five. The reason for this is simple, it receives and unifies all sensual data and directs an appropriate response when needed.

The number 5, *Heh* in Hebrew, represents *the archetype of universal life that plays the game of existence with the intermittent life-death process.* 5 is the first number in mathematical terms that is composed of both odd and even numbers, 2 the dyad, and 3 the triad. Interestingly, odd numbers were viewed as being well ordered and defined, as is the case with the trinitized 3. While even numbers were viewed as unresolved and therefore disorderly, due to the tension of opposites that is attributed to the first even number, which is 2. Actually, they are both part of a sequential unfoldment process, and therefore one cannot exist without the other. This beautifully illustrates the nature of man operating in the field of limitation, he is both resolved and unresolved - he is a unity but thinks he's not. Its solid geometrical form is the Pyramid, as in Egypt.

We come next to the number **6**. Six is the number of man becoming resolved. It is the number of spiritual man. This is where the things that are perceived of as being physical begin to merge with the things that are perceived of as being spiritual. Its symbolic representation is the six-pointed star, which is often called the *Star of David*. This comes about through the awakening (or activation) of the *6th Sense* that tells man that he is something more than the body. The number 6, *Vav* in Hebrew, expresses the archetype of the fertilizing agent, *that which impregnates or activates cosmically*. This is where man begins to understand the message of the six-pointed star, which is "*As Above, So Below.*" This is the place where the path of the 7 stones begins. All the steps actually take place between this number 6 and the next number in the sequence, which is the number 7. Mathematically, 6 is viewed as the first perfect number, though for a different reason than the number ten is viewed as perfect. Its solid form, geometrically, is the Cube. The Cube having six equal sides.

The number **7** is the number of the fully activated Unity. Here the perceptual view of what is physical and what is spiritual no longer exists. The two have become One, and the transformation has occurred. The concept of self and other has disappeared along with the illusion of time. This is where the *"One" is recognized as the many, and the many are recognized as the "One"*. The ancient Greeks referred to the number seven as the "*septenary*". To the Hebrews, 7, *Zayn*, is the number of unlimited possibility. Seven is the number of the Adept, the "**I AM That I AM**", it is the realm of *the Adam Kadmon*. Its biblical representation is the *7 Mighty Elohim*; the original Hebrew spelling which gives the value of **pi**, when read in its numerical form. (*Pi* being the name of the calculation that shows the ratio of the diameter to the circumference of a circle). The number seven is universal to most spiritual teachings; there are the seven souls of the Pharaoh, the seven sacred Rishis of the Hindus, the $7^{th}$ generation of the Native Americans, and far too many more to mention.

The mystic principle of the 7 is viewed as sacred, and can be used for many purposes. It is represented in the original 7 colours of Light in the solar spectrum, the 7 tones or notes of the musical scale, and the 7 main *Chakras* in the human body. Pythagoras called 7 the *Telesphoros* (the god of transformations, the one who brings completeness), because *by seven, all in the Universe and mankind is led to its end*; i.e., the end of the program of limitation. Here man, who is no longer just man (and never was), steps into the realm of the Infinite, where no boundaries exist. 7 is the number of the *Virgin Birth*; here the *Day of Judgment* has come and gone, and man has judged himself worthy. He has realized his true nature and deeply feels the essence of all that is, the essence of the One which he knows to be his own essence. He is no longer man. He is now the Adept who is *Self-Begotten*, and *Self-Sustaining*.

The Pythagoreans viewed the number seven as a spiritually perfect number, much the same as they did the number ten.  In mathematical terms the number *seven is the only number which*, (when) *multiplied by another number, creates none of the numbers in the Decad, and which cannot be created by the multiplication of any number*.  For this reason they gave it the name Athena, because the goddess was not born out of a mother and gave birth to none.  Symbolically it can be represented as a triangle over a square or a six-pointed star with a dot in the center.

The number **8** is the number of Infinity.  Here the Adept begins to learn how to use the science of harmonics as an energetic transmitting and receiving unit, within the greater structural body of the Universe.  This is Cosmic Man/Woman acting as a cellular unit of the *Universal Intelligence Network* or *Cosmic Brain*.  From here on out this and all further numbers are harmonics of the first 7 numbers, and can be viewed as variations on a theme.  Just as the eighth note of the musical scale is the octave of the first note, the number 8 here, is the harmonic octave of the Unity.  Mathematically eight is composed of Unity 1, and the septenary 7.  Symbolically it is represented as the horizontal figure eight, the Infinity sign, which represents the eternal spiraling motion of the cycles and shows the regular breathing of the Cosmos.

To the Hebrews the number 8 *Hhayt* represents the *primordial substance, the unfathomed reserve of undifferentiated, unstructured energy*.  Its plane geometrical shape is the octagon, and its solid shape is the stellated cube or Octahedron.  The octahedron is the shape of the oxygen molecule from which it takes its name, and is one of the shapes of the geometric type *Merkabah* (meditation vehicle).

The number **9** is the most secret and mysterious number of the ten number sequence. It is the highest, and the last whole number, and the first square number among the odd numbers. It is the *Trinitized Trinity* (three 3's), and *is the value of the degrees of every circumference of every circle*, i.e., **360 degrees: 3+6+0=9**. It seems to "*constantly reproduce itself in all shapes and figures through multiplication.*"[7]

It is usually only mentioned in the most veiled of terms, such as the Nine Storied Temple of Wisdom of the Free Masons, as well as other references in Norse and other mythologies. The Gnostics referred to the number 9 as the Ennead ('ninefold'), which refers to the great outer heaven of the universe. If you take the two, the three, and the four you will arrive at the nine, as the ancient Greeks would say. The number 9 is the number of completion, it is the point where the circle ends and begins anew, the Alpha and the Omega. It signifies the end of the old, in this case the program of self-limitation, and the beginning of the new that isn't actually new. The number 9 called Tayt in Hebrew represents receptivity and openness in the form of the *Feminine* archetype. Nine in the Hindu system is the number of the Goddess. The Goddess has 108 names, which in certain rituals are all recited four times - 4X108=432, 4+3+2=9, the number of the Goddess. It is called the sacred number of *Being and Becoming.*

These are the basic numbers, which are used in the formation of all further numerical combinations. These numbers have three levels of understanding in the Hebrew system. The 1st level, 1-9, represents the basic archetypes. The next 9 numbers of the 2nd level, 10-90, represent the manifestation of the archetypes in the everyday world. In the 3rd level the 9 numbers, 100-900, represent the motion of the numbers on a cosmic scale. Remember, "0" is a glyph that represents the eternal state of cosmic Be-ness. It only becomes a number when it is preceded by one of the numbers that follow it in the sequence.

Hopefully this will give you an idea as to why there seems to be so many numerical representations in almost every one of the ancient spiritual teachings. Most of these teachings are composed of two different, yet interrelated forms of language; one made up of letters, the other made up of numbers. If you don't know the meaning of one, you may not be getting the entire picture.

---

[7] The Secret Doctrine, H.P. Blavatsky, Theosophical University Press

# BACK TO THE EGO

Recognizing and understanding what the ego is, and what it does is very important if you wish to become liberated from the program of self-limitation. To begin with, **the ego is a programmed point of view** with a built-in survival mechanism, and not an actual thing per se. Its main function is one of constant comparison and separation. The original purpose of the thing that would later on become the present day ego, was to act as a sort of radar unit that was designed to help the body vehicle navigate within the greater body structure of the Universe; it came as standard equipment on all models. Its mechanical function was to keep the vehicle intact by informing it of potentially damaging situations, such as walking into a wall, or being in the path of a stampeding heard of Buffalo.

The ego comes into its present form when the sense of self is limited to the body vehicle only. When the limited sense of self is combined with the fully functioning mechanical navigation system, the main focus of attention becomes directed toward the survival of the self, the extent of which is perceived to be the body. This union of the two produces a very interesting energetic substance called *Fear*. Here we have another working example of the 2 giving birth to the third, only this time it's fear instead of Light. This is the reason the ego seems to have a life of its own. The ego believes that it is not only the protector of life, but too is the essence of that life itself.

The ego becomes very skilled at using the emotional body to maintain its survival by constantly separating itself (*you*) from, and then comparing itself to, everyone and everything it sees. It then makes judgment calls on those comparisons based on its own store of borrowed information, which like itself, is limited in amount as well as limiting in nature. In everyday life the ego sounds something like this - *I'm cool, they aren't. He/she has more than I do, and I want more, too. We're good, they're bad -- therefore, we are / I am better than they are. I'm right, you're wrong, I always... you never... you, you, I, I, me, me...* etc. etc. Sound familiar? Well, this is the language of the ego and it's pretty darn funny when you actually think about it. The predicament is that if you actually believe what the ego is saying, it sure doesn't feel very funny. These unfunny, or rather uncomfortable feelings are the direct result of the ego's manipulation of the emotional energy field.

It should be pointed out that the ego is the main thing that keeps the program of self-limitation in play. So basically, if you want to become unlimited, you should probably let go of the ego and its by-product, *fear* or; expand it to include <u>everything</u> in the universe! To effectively let go, we have to first recognize the way that the small ego sounds, and the way that those sounds feel.

Each one of those sounds or ego messages produces a sort of physical sensation in the body. The trick here is in learning how to observe those messages and their corresponding feelings without getting hung-up on them. This takes a certain amount of detachment. Up to this point, your relationship with the ego has been one of action/reaction. In other words, any time the ego made a move in the form of a thought/feeling, you immediately reacted to it. This action-reaction relationship is a sort of program that started to develop at a very young age by watching how other beings reacted to certain situations, and then imitating those reactions. Through repetition, the reaction has become habitual and therefore, a sort of program. There is a bit more involved with this, but the important thing here is to know that you are not your ego. Your survival does not depend on you having an ego. As a matter of fact, if you wish to continue with your development, it becomes very important that you do **not** have an ego. (EGO = Extremely Goofy Outlook.)

The general method of dealing with the feelings that are attached to the ego is to try to ignore them by stuffing them. This sometimes results in uncontrollable bouts of eating, drinking and/or shopping. If these options are unavailable, the result is usually something along the lines of screaming, shouting, fighting or crying. Usually there is a combination of at least two or more.

There are many more situations that are caused by the ego, some are a lot less comfortable than others - all involve some sort of fear. The most direct method of dealing with both ego and fear, is to simply take your attention off of the thought/message and re-focus it on the feeling or body sensation that accompanies it. Watch what it does, and where it's centered. It may move around or it might show up as a sort of tense feeling in the arms or neck. It might be a tight feeling in stomach or chest. Whatever it does, however it feels, keep your attention on it, and try to relax and breath into it. You will notice that these sensations are a lot like muscle cramps that are very tense at first, and then slowly start to relax more and more until they finally disappear altogether.

What happens when we avoid and deny these feelings, is that something like an energy feedback loop is created, which is centered around those feelings. Whatever amount of energy is used to avoid feeling them actually gets added to them so that the next time they come along, they're that much stronger. After a while they eventually become so strong that they can no longer be avoided, and we are pretty much forced to deal them. This is why some fears become so overwhelming, which can be extremely uncomfortable to say the least. The good news is that once we've learned how to deal with these sensations as soon as they arise, they become less and less intense, until they finally go away.

Another fairly direct way of dealing with the ego is to thank it for its assistance in enabling you to experience and understand limitation, and let it know that you no longer require its assistance. In the beginning it will most likely hang around for awhile and try to put its two cents worth in every chance it gets. Every time it does, simply say thank you for sharing, and go on with what you're doing. It will eventually get tired and either stop talking or go away completely.

This may sound a little nutty, but it actually works extremely well. (It also helps you to "lighten up" and not take yourself so seriously, which is really the point of the whole thing.) When we actually practice doing these things, we suddenly find that we are following the esoteric teachings of the Prajna-Patis (Lords of the Being) whose motto is "**Let us be gods and laugh at ourselves**." Interestingly, jokes themselves are a well-known example of spontaneous intuitive insight. In the split second where you understand a joke, you experience a moment of "enlightenment". One well loved Zen master's morning meditation actually consisted of 20 minutes of laughter. Even a line from the Tao Te Ching says: *"If it were not laughed at, it would not be sufficient to be Tao."* In other words, what ever you do, have fun with it.

The information being presented here is really nothing new. The Buddhists have spoken of these things for centuries. They call the line of information that comes from these higher frequency levels Prajna, which means: pure and unqualified knowledge, Enlightenment. In more basic terms it is called Super Knowledge.

There is really nothing that you need to do to be able to pick up these other frequencies except to let go of the ego. Keep your attention in the immediate vicinity of your body vehicle, which is always in the Now. Relax and become fully present with everything, just as it is. If any of the old thought patterns arise, observe them as if they were clouds and allow them to pass on through. Just be where you are. As you practice this you may begin to notice that the thought forms that present themselves are becoming very different than the ones you observed before you started practicing. Allow them to be there, and allow them to pass through, also. The idea being to quiet the mind, and allow yourself to have a full and complete experience of the ever present Now. Just the way it is at this moment. At first there may seem to be nothing particularly special about what's going on. However, as you continue you will begin to experience an incredible sense of precision and knowing in regard to the way the universe operates on a cosmic scale, as well as in your everyday life. If you're not sure how to do any of this there are hundreds of books available on this subject, some traditional, some not so traditional. Just find one that suits you and take it from there, though truthfully you don't really need any books, including the one you're reading right now... (Smile ☺)

# BROADCASTS AND THE BRAIN

O ne of the things that seems to have been forgotten during this last cycle is that we all share the same field of consciousness. (Well, actually we are the same field of consciousness.) Basically speaking, you're not the only one experiencing these sometimes bizarre thoughts. They're not really your thoughts per se. These thoughts actually exist as something that is very similar to a radio broadcast. A good example of this can be noted in the fields of scientific research and new inventions. It is a well-known fact that every time a new discovery in science is made, it is invariably made by several different and seemingly unrelated groups worldwide. This same phenomenon occurs with inventions as well. Everybody seems to come up with the same idea at the same time. There are many, many other broadcast frequencies in the general field of consciousness that are much more liberating, and much more entertaining than the ones some of us have been tuned in to of late. To be able to pick up these other broadcast frequencies you have to first let go of the one that you are listening to. This, once again, involves letting go of the ego (there's that ego word again). It is basically of limited nature, and is therefore limited as to what it can pick up.

The brain is the main organ through which these broadcast frequencies are filtered. Aside from its mechanical functions in regards to motor skills, it is an energy and information receiver and transmitter. Contrary to western belief, the brain is a function of consciousness, and not the source of it. In utilizing the numerical levels again, at **5**, the level of the body vehicle, the brain receives and interprets all sense data and transmits an appropriate response when one is required.

At level **6**, it begins to receive what it regards at first as extra-vehicular information pertaining to not only its role in relationship to the body vehicle, but its role in relationship to everything that it has up to this point regarded as extra vehicular, or other than itself. After working with, or rather, processing this information for a while, it then begins to perceive that *self and other* are quite possibly one and the same.

At level **7** it begins to explore its newly expanded role as a sort of cellular neuro-transmitter within the Greater Universal Intelligence Network, i.e., the Cosmic Brain. Here it realizes that, just as the body vehicle is made up of myriad cells all acting in synchronous harmony, it too plays a similar cellular type role within the greater body structure of the *Self* that is called the Universe. Here it begins to pick up and harmoniously direct the *Phowa* transmissions (broadcasts) of the Cosmic Intelligence, and in doing so, becomes a fully functioning cellular unit or member of the Universal Cosmic Intelligence Network. The U.C.I.N has many departments that govern many different functions such as matter formation and light reflection, formation and maintenance of all sorts of grids, density levels, transportation, intellectual, and intuitive development.

In more basic terms the brain is like a Ham radio set that is able to transmit as well as receive. Here, it is only able to transmit from the highest frequency that it is able to tune into. If it is operating in a limited low frequency range, it will transmit a low limited message. If it is capable of receiving a high frequency broadcast it will, whenever possible, transmit a high frequency message. Once again there is a little more to it than this, but this gives you a pretty good picture of what's occurring.

The dial on this radio is your attention. The more control you have of your attention, the higher the frequency level you can tune to. Interestingly, this dial or rather, your attention, also works as a two-way vibratory communication link between the body vehicle's perception center and whatever you're paying attention to. At a very basic level, any e-motional (*energy-motion*) that is transmitted along the line of this attention link is returned in kind. In other words, what you put out, you get back, sometimes much stronger. This is what lies behind the biblical saying: *What you sow, so shall you reap.*

In the field of limitation, this can become a sort of vicious circle that can get pretty hairy. It goes something like this - somehow the ego manipulates the emotional body enough to put you in a bad mood, therefore, if you're not careful you transmit that bad mood energy and it gets transmitted back to you in some fashion. This puts you in an even worse mood, which you then transmit out and... well, you get the picture. Remember, this works in both directions and you can become effected by another's output if you are still operating in the realm of separateness. If you multiply this some six billion times, and throw in some variations on the general theme such as fear, lack, selfishness, greed, and anger you have a pretty good horror film in the making. In energetic terms, what's happening here is a low frequency *entropic* feed back loop. (Entropic: from the word entropy, which refers to: the measure of decay and the degeneration of matter and energy.) From the standpoint of the ego, which is involved in this low frequency energy exchange, the Universe looks like a pretty scary place. From the standpoint of the Essential Self it all looks like everything is going according to schedule, which of course, it is.

Another scenario that you should probably be made aware of has to do with what occurs when you actively oppose something. The feed back loop that is created by your attention being focused on whatever it is that you oppose, coupled with the emotional energy that you use to oppose it, puts you in harmonic resonance or *faze* with that very thing - including limitation itself. This not only strengthens your connection to it, it actually empowers and perpetuates that situation. Sure, you may eventually win the supposed conflict but something else is bound to take its place and the cycle will then be repeated - usually around some other cause or in some other form - over and over again till you finally figure out what's going on. Once you are able to emotionally unplug from actively opposing limitation itself, and mindfully observe its effects, you will see that it is part of the Universal motion of expansion and contraction; expansion being limitless, and contraction being limited. They are both indicative of the regular breathing of the Cosmos.

The mindful observance of this process helps to keep you from becoming caught up in the illusion of duality, and effectively liberates you through the realization that they are both part of the same motion, and that neither can exist without the other. According to Shinzen Young, a fundamental error occurs when we become biased in favor of either of these aspects. This occurs when we view either of these aspects as being good or bad, or being better than the other. This type of view puts into play a subtle dynamic that presents us with a view of the world as being dualistic, therefore oppositional, and essentially antagonistic.

# FREQUENCY CHANGES

The word *frequency* here refers to the overall vibratory rate of a given signal. The frequency of a signal refers to how many times or how often a signal line moves, or rather, vibrates back and forth during a given period. This also has a direct correlation to the density of energy as matter.

One view is that the slower the movement, the lower the frequency, the less dense matter seems to become. The faster the movement, the higher the frequency, the more dense matter seems to become.

There is another view that says the opposite occurs. (See section on matter.) In terms of the evolution of consciousness, the more evolved it becomes, the faster it begins to vibrate - therefore its frequency rate becomes higher, though not necessarily denser. This is what some of our Native American Elders say is currently taking place here. The Earth is viewed by many as being in the process of taking a giant evolutionary leap forward, and its consciousness frequency is said to be moving to a higher level. This is what is being referred to by many as the Quickening, and the effects of this are being felt by many of us. If you are experiencing this phenomenon, the best way to deal with it is to simply keep your heart and your mind open. As a very wise and humorous Tibetan monk once said:

Don't be frightened, there's nothing to worry about, everything's going to be OK, you came in here in one piece, you're going to go out in the same way...

# MEDITATION

ow, the whole purpose behind the practice of meditation is to enable you to develop a sort of effortless control of your attention link. The practice of meditation teaches you the art of mindful, detached observance, which enables you to choose what part of the Self you plug into. The whole idea here is to have a mind that isn't constantly on guard against itself. The Hindus refer to this as living beyond *klesha*, which roughly translates to sticky mind. Alan Watts translates it as being, "the art of living without hang-ups". An interesting thing occurs once you've mastered the Ancient Secret Mystical Art of Living without Hang-ups, and it has to do with the effect you will have on everything around you.

The easiest way to understand this is to first look at everything as being a sort of sonic structure, which it actually is. In music for instance, when you play a stringed instrument such as a lute or a guitar, the plucking of a string sets up a vibratory motion that interacts with the air and produces a sound wave. The movement of this sound wave then interacts, to some degree, with everything it comes into contact with, including the eardrum, which picks up the vibration and transmits the signal to the brain. The brain then recognizes and translates the signal into audible sound. The intensity of the signal is what dictates how much effect the signal has on any given substance.

In the case of sound, the intensity of the signal is called its volume. Different sound vibrations or frequencies effect certain things differently. For instance, the right sonic frequency, projected at the right volume, can cause a glass to shatter through a process called harmonic resonance. In other words, the sound causes the glass to vibrate in such a way that the glass sets up its own vibration in response to the first vibration, and the combination of the two vibrational frequencies sets up an interference pattern that causes the glass to break. This type of occurrence can also be seen when you pluck a guitar string, and another one on an instrument across the room begins to vibrate without being plucked. At low volume this takes place because the string is tuned to a note that is in a similar or sympathetic frequency to the first note.

Bentov refers to this phenomenon as being a *resonant system* consisting of tuned *oscillators*. He goes on to explain that any number of oscillators that are in close proximity to each other, will eventually begin to oscillate at the exact same frequency.[8] At a higher volume all the other strings will begin to vibrate, regardless of whether or not they are in a sympathetic resonant frequency. This is all basically meant to point out the fact that vibratory motion not only has an effect on everything it comes into contact with, but that vibratory motion is what lies at the heart of all universal substance, seen and unseen. No matter what form it takes, all vibratory motion can essentially be viewed as "sound" or sonic structure.

Hence we get the ancient reference to the workings of the universe as being the Music of the Spheres.

You also have this same effect on everything because this type of motion takes place on all density levels, including the level of the *Phowa*. (Phowa: Tibetan word meaning: consciousness of light, the energizing intelligence of the Universe itself.) As Bentov explains:

"When we think, our brains produce rhythmic electric currents. With their magnetic components, they spread out into space at the velocity of light, as do the electric waves or sounds produced by our hearts. They all mingle to form enormous interference patterns, spreading out and away from the planet. They are admittedly weak, but they are there. The more finely our systems are tuned, the clearer a signal we can pick out of the general noise and jumble of sounds" (vibrational frequencies).

Once we are consciously able to connect up with these Phowa transmissions through our attention link, we can begin to develop a working relationship with the source of the transmission. Depending on the point of view, that source can often seem to consist of any number of interrelated transmission points, or beings, all sharing the same frequency of consciousness who use that frequency as a recognition code. These transmissions are easily recognized through the manner in which the information is presented. It is always unconditional, open, and non-judgmental, it is allowing and respectful of your free will, it doesn't want anything and it doesn't participate in bargaining of any sort, it gives what it has freely and asks for nothing in return. It is all-inclusive, very loving, and quite often very humorous. If you happen to come into contact with an information line that doesn't present itself in this fashion, it's your choice as to whether you pay attention to it or not.

This consciousness frequency has been known by many different names throughout the ages. It is sometimes referred to as the Shema Yisrael in Hebrew, and said to be used for the quickening of the People of Light. It is the vibration of complete and total unlimited freedom. Connection to this source effectively turns you into a sort of high frequency transmitter whose signal gets radiated out and effects everything and every one around. You in essence become a "Light unto the world", and you will actually effect not only the level of conscious awareness, but also the vibratory structure itself. This includes your own body vehicle.

The Shema Yisrael can be likened to a sort of ultra sonic frequency along which the Phowa transmissions are carried. In this case, the Shema acts like a kind of open standing carrier wave that becomes active when it is modulated by the transmission of the Phowa. The two acting as a single process are totally inseparable.

At the level of the body vehicle, the combined action of the Phowa-Shema transmission can help to activate certain of the dormant strands within the **DNA** structure. This occurs through a process that involves *nested* or non-interfering electro-magnetic waves that emanate from the Heart center. These nested, or rather, harmonious waves are able to transfer this harmonic resonance through the principle of *hydro-dynamics* to the blood, which carries it through out the body. At the same time, this hydrodynamic resonance sort of massages the DNA and enables it to become more tightly braided (which is what actually helps connect and activate the dormant strands). Thus enabling the body to work more readily within a higher frequency range, and with a higher valency of Inner Light through the increased production of *serotonin* and *melotonin* in the brain; this is also a result of this process.

Science has known for quite a while now, that the production and assimilation of *seratonin* in particular, has a very strong effect on the level of awareness. Such substances as mescaline - the active agent in peyote, a sacred medicine to many Native Americans - and LSD, (which neuro-science no longer views as mere hallucinogens, but as consciousness enhancing substances), are themselves *serotonergic agonists.* Both of these substances produce similar effects on the firing rate of serotonergic neurons, and on the level and rate of turnover of serotonin in the brain. According to current scientific research, these substances both share the same indolealkylamine structure as serotonin, and act upon the same physical mechanisms or receptors in the brain, i.e. - the 5-HT2 receptors. These 5-HT2 receptors are of particular interest to scientists currently involved in the neurological study of the brain because of their multifaceted actions in the body, and the importance of their function for mental and physical health.[9]

The activation of dormant DNA strands have been noticed in humans who have experienced what is loosely called miraculous healings. This and many other documented genetic mutations form the basis for the emerging medical studies whose main focus is to map human genetic mutations. Genetic research involving the HIV virus points out the overall *natural resiliency* and *adaptability* of the human organism. Scientists have recently found a genetic mutation that occurs in the CCR5 gene. "The CCR5 gene encodes a protein on human immune cells that helps HIV enter and infect those cells. Recent studies have shown that individuals who produce mutant forms of CCR5 protein are more likely to resist HIV infection or have slower HIV disease progression than individuals who produce normal CCR5 protein." [10]

Other studies indicate that the activation of normally dormant strands within the DNA structure seems to occur when one adopts an attitude of calm centeredness, and is no longer afraid of the illusion of death. This also tends to eliminate the matter of stress as well. Basically, the body/consciousness is moved into a slightly higher frequency, and is no longer effected by the lower operational frequency of dis-ease.

The on going effects of being able to keep our attention linked within the higher frequency is that it will eventually bring us into the conscious presence of the source of that transmission, the very source of our own essence. In other words, our attention link is a sort of Jacob's Ladder.

It should be reiterated that the body plays a very important role in all of this, and that you fully accept being associated with it while you are here. It contains your processing net work, and is your main base of operations, around which your conscious aspect is focused. All the information needed to assist you on your journey is encoded within its cellular and energetic structure. (Chelsea Flor teaches a much more detailed understanding of this concept.)

In many of the ancient and current teachings, the body is viewed as a manifestation of the universal mind, and is seen as the key to the mystical experience of the world. In the words of Tibetan Lama Govinda:

To the enlightened man whose consciousness embraces the universe, to him the universe becomes his body, while his physical body becomes manifestation of the universal mind, his inner vision an expression of eternal truth...

---

[8] Stalking the Wild Pendulum, Itzhak Bentov, Pg. 23-25, Destiny Books, Publisher, 1977
[9] NIDA Research Monograph Series 146 * Hallucinogens: An Update, Pg. 92-116, 1994
[10] National Institute of Allergy and Infectious Diseases, national Institutes of Health, News Release, Sept. 23, 1998

# ACADEMY OF UR

# GRADE 3:

# Application of Ancient Physics

# Pyramids, Merkabah and the Octahedron

So far everything in this text has been, for the most part, fairly basic although at times a bit wordy. The intended purpose of the way this information is being presented is to bring together as many seemingly unrelated, but significant aspects of the universe as possible in order to show its true interrelated nature. This is a sort of non-linear *gathering of the sparks* process that will continue throughout the remainder of the text. I hope that by presenting the information in the language of Spiritual/science, that there will be less chance of it being misinterpreted. Although in truth, the use of any verbal based language is highly inadequate in any attempt to describe the workings of the universal consciousness. This is because of its inherent built-in limitations that are unable to take into account, much less explain the other *essential*, non-verbal means of communication.

What is here though, is intended to stimulate the intellectual part of what is commonly referred to as your *spiritual nature*, by focusing the wandering analytical aspect of the consciousness in such a way that it is always brought back to a view of the inherent unity of all things. This works quite well because of the simple fact that whatever you see to be true, is essentially the way you will begin to experience things.

To paraphrase a not so ancient master:

*"The higher spiritual progress can at times be greatly enhanced when accompanied by intellectual development on a parallel line."*[11]

This also applies to the development of the intuitive aspect of the intellect as well. Whether we are able to understand something analytically or not, we should all try looking at things from an intuitive level as well - it is there that we are most likely to find a deeper level of understanding.

All of this information is intended to stretch the boundary lines of the limited conceptual / consensual reality, and bring the focus of attention into the fully functioning experiential reality level of the *Now*. The intention is to boost or kick-start the awakening process of the consciousness, which during the last part of this cycle seems, for the most part, to have been asleep.

An important thing to remember here is that you will only get out of something as much as you put into it. This should be kept in mind as we begin this particular section, the intended purpose of which is to help bring the center of operation out of the head, and into the Heart center. This is where the decision making process is taken out of the hands of the limited intellectual grasp of the ego and turned over to the *still, small inner voice* of the Heart center, thus enabling the development of the higher intuitive/intellectual process to take place. This will involve the construction of a Merkabah using good, old fashion, everyday thought-form technology. This includes visualization and meditation, which utilizes the Super-Luminal properties of thought.

The Merkabah tradition itself, while treated by some as being relatively new, can actually be traced back to somewhere around 500 to 1000 BC (Remember, that too is a linear perception.)

It should probably be pointed out that the Merkabah meditation being presented here is by no-means traditional. The only reason it is being presented at all is because it works. If you so choose, you can add your own breathing technique to the meditation as well as anything else that you think might be helpful; Mundras (Eastern meditative hand gestures), pinball, juggling, what ever. As was said before, there is no one right way of doing any of this.

A Merkabah is a spiritual vehicle sometimes referred to as a moving "Throne" or "Chariot" according to Ezekiel 1:4-28, although in the biblical Hebrew accounts the *Merkabah* מרכבה is referred to as a *Rekev* רכב which simply means; Vehicle. Hurtak describes a Merkabah as:

> "A Divine Light vehicle used by the Masters to probe and reach the faithful in the many dimensions of the Divine Mind. The Merkabah can take on many forms of a brilliant Briolette in the physical worlds."[12] (A Briolette: a gem having its entire surface cut with triangular facets.)

Chelsea Flor further explains a Merkabah as a:

> "Vehicle consisting of Super-Luminal properties of pre-state particles of light. It is constructed of geometrical grids that are crystalline in nature, and of various shapes and dimensions. The shape

and dimension of the Merkabah itself is solely dependent upon the evolutionary stage of the consciousness using the vehicle." [13]

This particular Merkabah is in the shape of an Octahedron, also referred to as a Delta T configuration, that consists of 13 points. 6 outer points and 7 inner points with 8 outer triangular surfaces which give the outward appearance of a Diamond. This formation will essentially become a sort of command center from which you will be able to direct the functions of this and other similar unfoldments of the geometrical forms of the Merkabah. Remember, the word Merkabah simply means vehicle. The Buddha himself referred to the Eightfold path as a vehicle also, which makes it a type of Merkabah itself.

In essence, anything that is capable of bringing you to a heightened state of universal or spiritual awareness can be viewed as a Merkabah. In its most basic form the number 6 represents the manifest world in the form of the 6 directions; up, down, left, right, front, back, though this view is soon to become greatly expanded. 6, as was mentioned before, is the number of awakening man. It is also the atomic number of carbon, the structure of which is: 6 electrons, 6 protons and 6 neutrons. (666?) It becomes real interesting when you realize that man is considered to be a carbon based life form. It becomes even more interesting when we see that the Hebrew word that was translated in the Bible as meaning "beast", can also be translated as meaning "enclosure". Now, if the body is thought to be the robe or the enclosure of the Soul and... well, you get the idea.

The number 7 represents the seven energy centers of the body that are formed when all Ten Sephiroth in the Qabalistic Tree of Life are balanced along the center path of the three vertical paths or pillars. Depending on which representation of the Tree of Life is being used, you can come up with as many as 9 vertical energy centers as in the *Gra*[14] version, which is the number we will be using later on. These are the same energy centers that are called Chakras in the eastern tradition. They are also the 7 Great Seals spoken of in the biblical texts. Seven is the number of transformation, and the atomic number of nitrogen.

The number 8 is the number of infinity, which is the realm of limitlessness. 8 is the number of oxygen whose elemental form is the cube. It is the element of the breath. Here the lower cubic form becomes transformed by the evolving consciousness into its next level of unfoldment, the stellated cube or Octahedron, which forms the matrix of the Merkabah. Through the use and understanding of this form and its corresponding inner grid, the breath is transformed to the next level of unfoldment that is sometimes called the *Ruach Adonai* אדני רוח - *The Divine Breath or Spirit of God.*

To bring in a Buddhist analogy, the Octahedron itself can essentially become a vehicle of the eight-fold path. The main function of this vehicle is to balance the energy centers of the body in order to bring the consciousness back into a fully functioning state of unity, or 1-ness. Interestingly, the number 1 is the atomic number of Hydrogen, which is the main bonding element of all atomic structure. As you may have noticed, we now have all four of the elements that form the basic building blocks of all life contained in the numerical sequence that goes into the construction of the Merkabah.

The number 13 has many significant numerical aspects. In Hebrew, 13 is the number of Ahbah אהבה, the word for Love, and is also the number of Achad כאחד, which means unity. When these two are added together, they produce the number 26. This is the number of YHVH יהוה. YHVH (or YHWH): Yod - Hey - Vav - Hey, is the unspeakable sacred name of God. One of the reasons it is unspeakable is because it is more of a numerical/spiritual equation and not a name per se. 13 is the number of the lunar

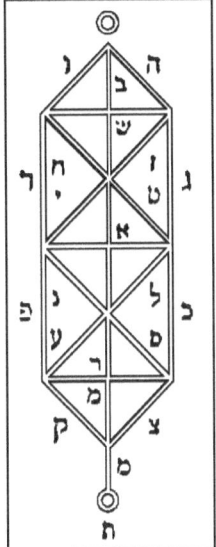

cycles and forms the basis of the Mayan calendar. In Christian terms, 13 is represented in the twelve disciples plus the Christ.

It should be pointed out that each of these numbers have many more significant aspects than the ones presented here, and that you can use any aspect that you feel is appropriate, and as many as you like. In fact, it is not necessary that you understand the numerical aspects at all in order to use this form, (although they are quite helpful). The point being that this is a tool of liberation and freedom, so use it as freely as you choose. It is yours and it belongs to everyone.

This meditation is very much like a *Medicine Wheel* with the 4 lateral points being set like the 4 directional doors of North, South, East, and West. Here though, the center is you. For the direction of Above, you can use Creator, Great Spirit, or Undifferentiated Cosmic Continuum, whatever works for you. For purposes of continuity we will refer to it as *Ain Soph* אין סוף, The Limitless Light. For the direction Below, you can use Earth, Terra, Logos, once again whatever you choose. Here we will use the ancient Hebrew term *Malkuth* מלכות, which means Kingdom, sometimes referred to as the World of Foundation or the Sphere of the Elements.

The important thing is that you map out the 6 directions of the seemingly physical world, with you at the center. Next, we come to the 7 energy points within the body vehicle. There are actually many more, but we are going to use the 7 main points, or Chakras, here by aligning them vertically with the 2 points Above and Below, and horizontally through the heart center, with the 4 lateral directional points of front, back, left and right.

Visualize a line or ray of light coming from the point Below that runs through the body and through the 7 inner Chakra points, and connects up with the point Above. This gives us our vertical axis. Next, visualize a line or ray of light running horizontally through the Heart center from back to front, and then repeat the process, only this time the ray or line will

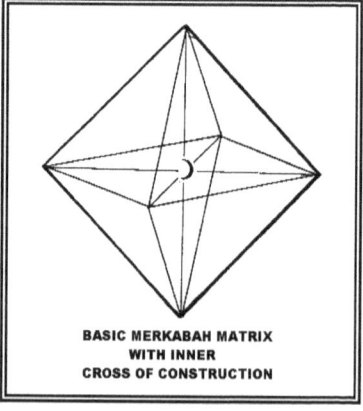

BASIC MERKABAH MATRIX
WITH INNER
CROSS OF CONSTRUCTION

go through the Heart center from left to right. (It doesn't matter what direction you start the lines from, as long as they are there). This gives us the framework to construct the rest of the Merkabah. Next, we will connect up the 2 points that are Above and Below with the 4 lateral points. This gives us a basic Diamond shaped outer structure. (See illustration)

Before we go on to the construction of the inner grid formation of the Merkabah, it should be pointed out that this diamond shaped energy form already exists around the body and is sometimes referred to as the Crystalline Energy Grid. All we are doing here is bringing it into focus, and learning how to access it. The easiest way to understand the form of this

energy field is to imagine 2 large Pyramids of light with one coming from the Earth, and the other coming from the Sky, the points of which are overlapping, or rather merging. This overlapping section is what forms the shape of the diamond, and in the middle of that diamond is you.

The lower Pyramid coming from the Earth and pointing toward the Sky is the I AM Pyramid of Man in his/her seeming state of separation. The upper Pyramid coming from above and pointing toward Earth is the I AM Pyramid of the *Essential Self*

(Universal Consciousness, Great Spirit, **YHVH, and God etc.**) By working with this formation we will be consciously merging our energy with the higher vibratory frequencies of the upper Pyramid, which is our true aspect. This serves to put us in a natural "Tuned Oscillation" with our own higher source of intelligence, and allows *Klesha* type resonance to be removed.

The next step is to connect the remaining inner Chakras to the four lateral points by visualizing 4 lines or rays of light coming from each one of the Chakras, and connecting to each of the 4 lateral points. Including the lines that form the outer structure, this gives us a series of 8 Pyramids, 4 ascending and 4 descending, of varying heights all sharing the same base line at the level of the Heart. This completes the basic Merkabah Grid formation, and we will now move on to an expanded view of some of the significant aspects of this form.

---

[11] Excerpt from a private letter to H.P. Blavatsky from one of the beings she refers to as the "Mahatmas".

[12] J. Hurtak, Book of Knowledge-the Keys of Enoch, 1973

[13] Excerpt from personal conversations with Chelsea Flor.

[14] Sefer Yetzirah, Gra Version, Warsaw, 1884 Edition

# MORE NUMBERS AND OTHER STUFF

ow we are going to go back and examine the lines and points that went into the construction of our Merkabah. The lines that lie at the center of the Grid that we used as the foundation for our outer matrix, or octahedron are represented by the last letter in the Hebrew alphabet Tau ת. Tau means: Cross, foundation, framework of construction. This cross in its basic form represents the cross of space-time upon which limited man is crucified. When the full implications of what stands behind this cross are realized, it then has the ability to become the "Cross of Liberation".

The lines that we used to connect the 4 lateral points are represented as; **a)** the time line, running from back to front: back being the past and front being the future; and **b)** the polarity line, running from side to side. This represents the polar aspects of consciousness that can be most easily recognized as Yin and Yang. Yin represents the intuitive nature of consciousness. Yang represents the analytical nature of consciousness. In terms of the brain, Yin which is referred to as being on the left, is represented as being the intuitive function of the right brain, and Yang which is on the right, is represented as being the analytical function of the left brain. This is what is being described when someone is referred to as either left brained or right brained. In truth, we all have equal amounts of both of these aspects, though one may be more developed than the other. The optimal point of balance is achieved through the full development and integration of both aspects. If we go back and look at the principle of opposing dynamics, the tension that is released by the full integration of the two gives birth to the third in the form of Self Illumination, or *en-light-enment*.

The time line as represented by the aspects of past and future is a little more complicated to explain because... well, basically... it doesn't actually exist, at least not in the way that we usually think of it. Time is a system of measurement that is used to calculate the change and movement of observable bodies within a given space, and the two cannot be separated. Space is not 3 dimensional, and time is not a separate entity. Both are completely interrelated, and form a 4 dimensional continuum, called space-time. In that sense it exists, but not separately. The only access we have to anything remotely resembling a point of time is 'Now'. All actions take place in the Now.

All observations of the past, and all speculations on the future take place in the Now. Time is basically a relative point of view that is totally dependent upon the point or space from which an observation is made. Let's say for instance that you are in orbit around the Earth. In a matter of a couple of hours you are able to experience something that it takes the people on Earth 24 hours to experience, namely a full rotation of the planet. So in other words, time is a relative form of measurement that is interdependent upon space, and not an actual fixed separate thing.

Interestingly, the more prevalent linear perception of time is one of the main things that has allowed us to participate in the program of limitation. In its most simplistic function the linear perception of time works in such a way that it is able to keep our attention focused on the non-active points of the space-time line. The non-active points are; tomorrow or later on; something that has not yet come to be, and yesterday, that which was experienced earlier (or at least what the memory perceived that experience to be) though is no longer. This has had the tendency to keep the attention focused on one end of the time line or the other, and off of the only truly active point, which is the ever present 'Now'. As we look at our space-time line, we have one end that represents the past, and one end that represents the future. In the middle of that line, where the polar line crosses the space-time line, is the point that represents the Now. This is also the place where the vertical line crosses the two lateral lines, which is also the Heart Chakra, the point of Balance.

# Seven to Nine

To give us an expanded view of our relationship to the Cosmos, all of the points along the vertical axis will be referred to as Chakras, thus expanding the number of Chakras from 7 to 9. Here a slightly different view of what each Chakra represents will be given.

Because of the expanded level of connection that occurs between all of the Chakras through the use of this Grid, all 13 points take on the function of being Chakra centers and will essentially begin to function as One. In order of ascension, the 1st Chakra is called *Malkuth* מלכות (i.e. Kingdom), and it is the Earth. We see this as the foundation of our bodies. It is very important that we keep this in mind while we're here. Our entire life function at this time is completely dependent upon the Earth. It supplies every single thing that is needed in order to keep our body vehicles functioning. We are a part of it, and it is a part of us. It is the Mother of all terrestrial life forms. Our bodies are one of the ways in which the entire universe expresses itself, and that expression takes place as an integral process of the Earth's life producing function.

Basically, she's part our life support system, and we are part of hers, so we might want to think about taking some responsibility for our own actions in the way that we treat Her, if you haven't already. Remember that we are not responsible for anyone else's actions. This only serves to involve us in a line of action that we may not be able to easily extricate ourselves from, and does a disservice to the other party. We may only help when asked, and then, at our own discretion. Remember the "Non-interference Directive" from Star Trek? Well, there really is one!

We will call the 2<sup>nd</sup> Chakra *Ahbah* אהבה Love. This is the Chakra that is commonly referred to as the Root, which makes perfect sense because at the Root of all existence stands Love.

The 3<sup>rd</sup> Chakra we will call *Ur* אור, which means Light. This is where the Light of the emerging consciousness enters the body vehicle through the portal of the umbilicus.

The 4<sup>th</sup> Chakra is the Center of Peace; *Shalom* שלום. It is the area of the solar plexus (the former Chakra of control, in regards to ego based man). This is where man, who is now Divine man, has ceased the struggle for control, and has surrendered the *Nephesh* נפש (lowest part of the tripartite soul, i.e. ego) to the *Yonah Shalom* Dove of Peace for delivery into the realms of the Higher Self. This is the meaning behind the biblical word Deliverance. Man is delivered from the program of self-limitation, which is the cross of space-time and is now ready to participate in the next level of unfoldment.

The 5<sup>th</sup> Chakra is the Heart Center and is represented by the Hebrew letter *Aleph* א, which is the symbol of "Unity and Oneness". The placement of the א (the 1<sup>st</sup> letter of the Hebrew alphabet) over the *Tau* ת (the last letter of the Hebrew alphabet which represents the Merkabah's Cross of Construction), gives us the key to decoding the mystery of the Alpha/Omega and brings us to the end of program of limitation.

Application of Ancient Physics          79

The 6th Chakra is the area of the throat, and is the Center of Harmony. It is represented by the Hebrew word *Qol* קול, which means: *Voice*. Here the 6th Chakra harmoniously interacts with all the other Chakras, and becomes the Voice of "The Many as The One".

The 7<sup>th</sup> Chakra is the Center of Truth and is signified by the 16<sup>th</sup> (1+6=7) letter of the Hebrew alphabet *Ayin* ע, which means Eye. This represents the fully developed Third Eye or penial gland, which is involved in the manufacture of serotonin. It is able to see the Perfect Beauty that is Truth.

The 8<sup>th</sup> Chakra is Freedom, which is the *Kether* כתר or Crown. It is represented by the phrase *Ehyeh Asher Ehyeh: I AM That I AM*. This is the Freedom that comes through the recognition of the absorption and fusion of individual identity into the Divine Identity of the Essential Self.

The 9th Chakra is Ain Soph אין סוף, Infinity (without limit) - The Light that sees and knows itself to 'Be' - The Light Continuum which is the Universal Self.

The number of lines or rays that emanate from the Chakra centers along the vertical axis to the 4 lateral directional points is 36. In one of his dialogs on Desire the Buddha says, "*Thirty-six streams are rushing toward you.*" This number represents a collective vibrational frequency that is directly related to Earth-based mankind's consciousness. When these 36 streams are not balanced along the Heart line, our general experience is one of random chaos. When balance is achieved, we are gently lead into another level of conscious awareness.

In traditional Hebrew terms, the 36 is represented in the form of the 36 beings or saints that are present in the world at all times called *Tzadiq-Hem* צדיק הם, which translates to: Righteous They or Them. According to Hurtak:

> "These 36 are able to go directly into the presence of the "Throne" center for programs of creation, in order to ascertain the sequence involved in program manifestation".[15]

Collectively, they hold and maintain the universal "I AM" frequency of the Earth on a conscious level. In the Eastern tradition these beings are also known as *Bodhisattvas*. By working with the information presented here we are able to bring our own frequency into direct alignment with the balanced flow pattern of the 36 (3+6=9). (See illustration on next page.)

Because this action takes place within the zone that is formed by the merging of the two "I AM" Pyramidal light or energy structures, the frequency of the lower structure becomes modulated by the higher frequency of the upper structure, allowing for natural phase-resonance to occur between the two. This creates a flow pattern that allows the 9 vertical Chakra centers to take on an expanded role, and function as:

> "9 major mechanisms of the physical overlap between the different evolutionary levels." [15]

The complete frequency alignment of both the upper and lower structures allows them both to spin, thus taking on the aspect of a high spinning octahedron or twin vortex, the action of which occurs naturally.

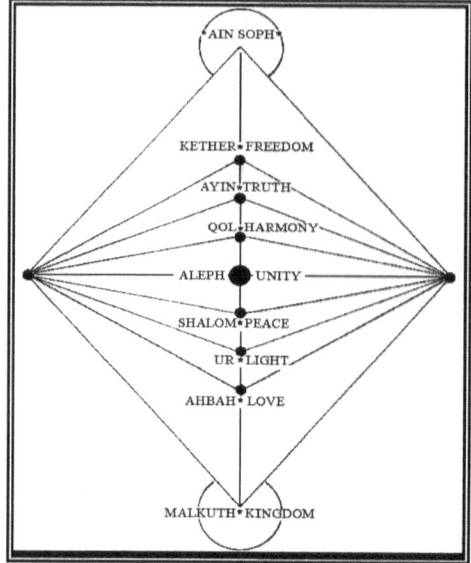

Here, because of the directional flow of the energy of each structure, the as-pects of the 1st and 9th Chakra are combined and extended to the 4 lateral points. They each take on the combined aspect of the two, thus making them all the *Kingdom of Infinite Light.* The same holds true for the other Chakras as well, 2 and 8 becoming *Freedom of Love,* 5 and 7 becoming *Light of Truth,* and 4 and 6 becoming *Harmony of Peace*, with the Heart Chakra remaining the *Center of Unity.* All are directly connected to the Kingdom of Infinite Light. This also changes the active nature of our original 13 points of construction to 26, the number of YHVH.

When the 36 frequency of the upper structure and the 36 frequency of the lower structure become fully matched or phase-locked, they create an overall frequency of 72. This is represented in the Merkabah as the *Shem ha-Mephorash* המפרש שם "Name of Extension", and specifically refers to the 72-fold name of God contained in the original Hebrew version of Exodus 14:19-21. In essence, the Merkabah is the vehicle of the Exodus, allowing man, who is no-longer just man, to take his/her Exodus from the lower realms of self-limitation. By adding his/her name with the Seal of his Breath (i.e. his frequency) to the list of names in the Shem ha-Mephorash he/she enters the "House of Many Mansions", the next level of the virtual reality game.

---

[15] J. Hurtak, Book of Knowledge; The Keys of Enoch, 1973

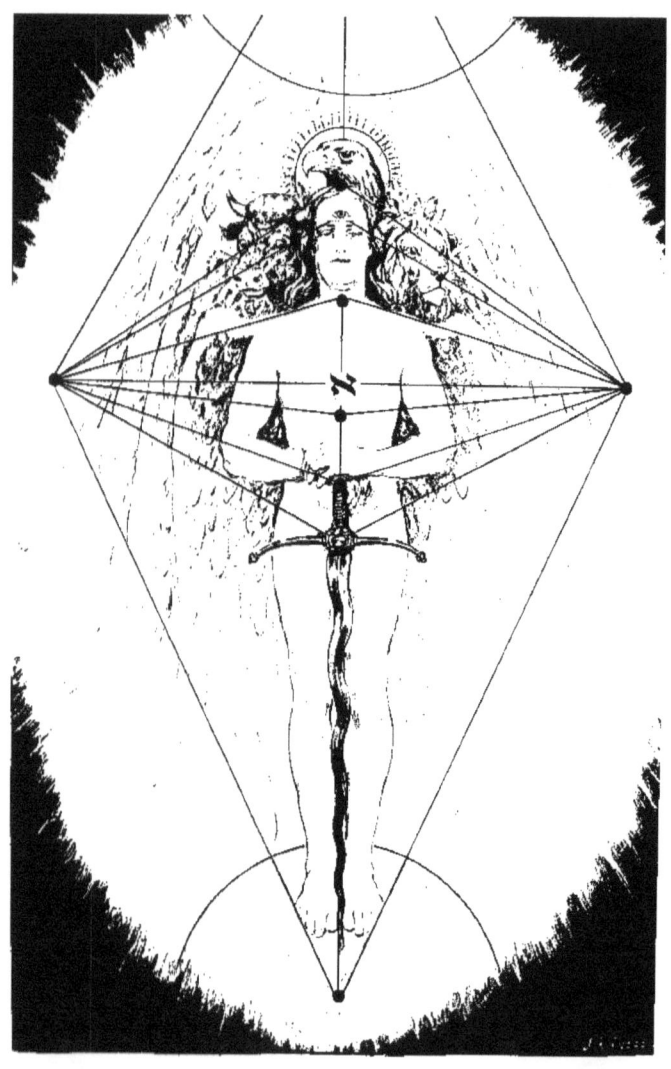

# Geometric Information

his information should allow you to work more effectively with the further unfoldments of the Merkahbic form. The unfoldment pattern starts in the pre-matter state with the Octahedron and follows a very non-linear path. One way of understanding this is to imagine that there is a line dividing pre-matter from matter. According to Chelsea Flor, the first movement takes place on the pre-matter side of the line and can most easily be described as a 3-axis sub-quark particle motion, which translates geometrically in to the form of an Octahedron. These sub-quarks are actually Anu particles or God particles. These particles are what make up the super-luminal properties of Divine Thought, or what the Tibetans call the Phowa.

The next movement takes place on the matter side of the line as the first matter state unfoldment which is a Tetrahedron, the next unfoldment of which, is the Cube, also takes place on the matter side of the line.

The next unfoldment presents itself as a Unity model based on its 3-axis spin rotation which shows its center to be a perfect zero point and is a stellated Cube Octahedron/Diamond. Now this unfoldment takes place directly on the line between pre-matter and matter (or if you like, Spirit & matter) and essentially dissolves the line completely by unifying both aspects into the One. Also, if you rotate a vertically standing transparent Octahedron backwards or forwards 23.5 degrees you will see that it forms a perfect Star of David or as the Knights Templers called the it, *The Gem*.

Mathematically the next form, the stellated Octahedron that is nowadays called a Star-tetrahedron, presents itself as a duality model based on its spin axis rotation and its dual male-female nature. Although in linear terms it is a more advanced geometric form, the Star-tetrahedron is actually experienced before the Octahedron and is representative of the awakening, but still duality based, consciousness of mankind. Now what's happening here is really very interesting, though a little tough to explain. This is due to the non-linear nature of the unfoldment pattern, as it relates to the current status of Earth based human consciousness. What actually happens is that the geometric forms unfold around each other from the center outward.

**5 SIDED PYRAMID**

**STAR-TETRAHEDRON**

**OCTAHEDRON**
SLIGHTLY ROTATED TO SHOW
STAR OF DAVID

The 1st Octahedron represents the awakening, primordial, cosmic consciousness.

The next stage is where that primordial consciousness finds itself in the world of temporal continuity called matter. This is represented as an Octahedron inside of, or rather, surrounded by a Tetrahedron, which as we saw earlier, represents matter. This is analogous to the newborn that suddenly finds itself in the world.

The next unfoldment is the Cube, which represents the development of self-awareness in the form of the ego or limited sense of self.

In the next sequence the Cube is surrounded by another Octahedron which in turn, is itself, surrounded by what is sometimes called a Star-tetrahedron (2 interlocking Tetrahedrons). The space at the center of these 2 interlocking forms (the Octahedron) is called *The Diamond Heart.*

Here's the point: The developing consciousness skips the Octahedron, which is the Unity stage, and instead, goes directly to the seemingly bi-polar duality stage of consciousness represented by the Star-tetrahedron. In order for the consciousness to make any sense out of this seemingly duality based world, it has to sort of take a step back, or in this case, *go inside of itself* to find the key. Once the key is found, the duality aspect of the Universe that was originally thought to be represented by the Star-tetrahedron, is seen instead as representing a dynamic aspect of the process of creation that is dyadic or triadic in nature, and by no means dualistic.

This action in itself not only represents the sort of back & forth pulsating motion that is exhibited by the entire Cosmos, it also beautifully illustrates the fundamental message that lies at the heart of all the ancient spiritual teachings: *if you want to find the answer, look inside of yourself.*

Now, it should be pointed out that these forms serve many, varied functions and depending on the context in which they are being used, they can unfold in various ways, particularly if rotation is added to the unfoldment sequence. The important thing to remember is that these shapes all co-define each other. They represent Universal archetypes of motion and affinity, and they are essentially metaphorical. This is but one way of looking at them. They are not however, meant to form the bases of a new belief system or reinforce an already existing one. As you already may know, belief of one thing implies disbelief of another and disbelief is a form of self limitation, which is something we are learning to let

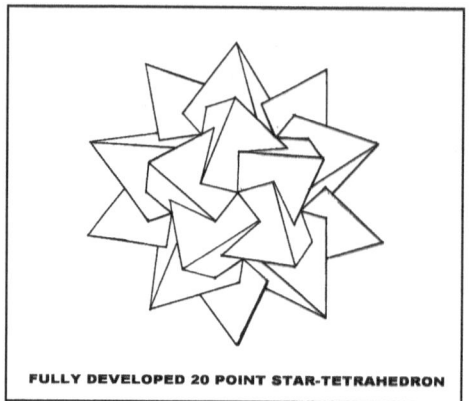

**FULLY DEVELOPED 20 POINT STAR-TETRAHEDRON**

go of, not trying to create more of. You're not being asked to believe any of this or anything else for that matter. Just look at it and see if any of it rings true. If and when you find that this information has helped you along the path of liberation, it too should be let go of.

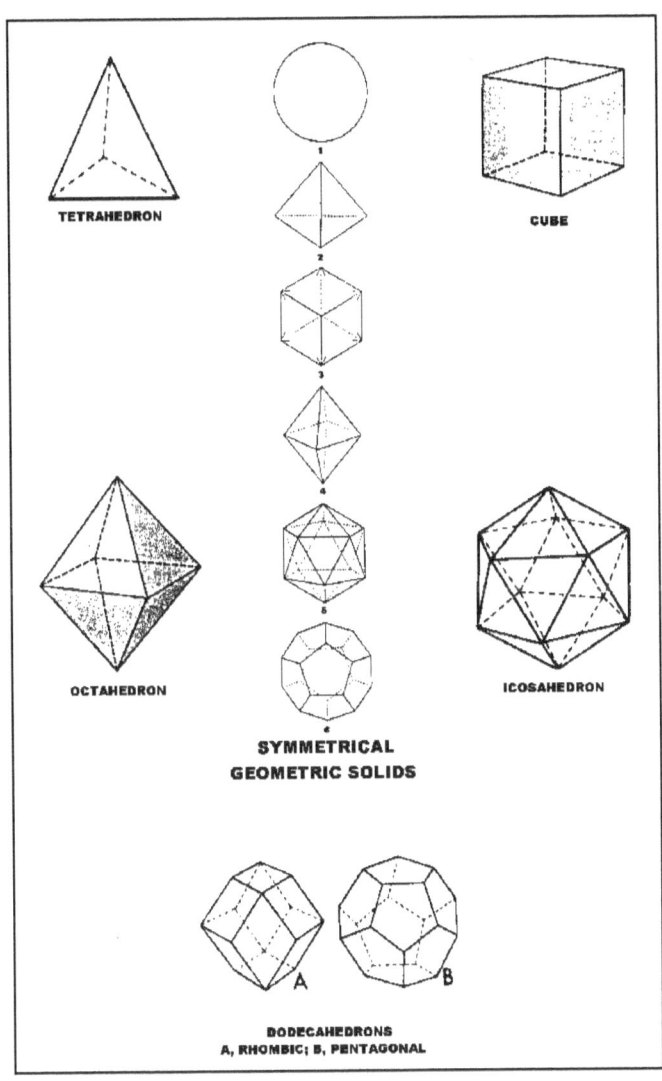

# WHY AN OCTAHEDRON?

The ancient initiates seemed to have felt that the Octahedron was important. We can see this quite clearly if we are diligent in our inquiries into the ancient spiritual schools and texts. We seem to be constantly presented with information that, although at times is quite veiled, either alludes to or directly presents us with this shape. In order to see these things, we find that we have to go beyond what we are told and look at them for ourselves. At times, the dogma that seems to surround some of the more traditional schools of thought and methods of teaching can get in the way of our being able to clearly understand just what is being presented to us. Though the dogma can be a hindrance to us if we're not careful, it none the less serves a very important function, which is to keep the body of knowledge intact as a whole. In essence, the dogma acts as a sort of watchdog that we have to learn how to get past in order to see what lies at the heart of the matter (watch dog-ma?)

The most easily recognizable representation of the principle of the Octahedron being used in a spiritual context is the Medicine wheel of the Native Americans. The 6 directions of North, South, East, West, Above & Below are indicative of the 6 points of the Octahedron, with the center focal point being Great Spirit, Creator or You.

Another example is presented to us in the ancient Hebrew text known as the **Sepher Yetzirah**, which translates, to *Book of Formation* or the *Book of Creation*. There are several versions of this book that are known to exist and much speculation as to the origin of each. The word *sepher* itself is thought by some, to be the origin of the English words *cipher* and *sphere*.

In chapter IV, verse 3, of the Gra version of the **Sepher Yetzirah**,[16] we find the following:

> "Seven Doubles: Vayt, Ghimel, Tayt, Khaf, Phay, Raysh, Tav as in the presents of Seven extremities, six of which - height, depth, East, West, North and South - and the holy sanctuary (which) directs them from the middle, and it is the Aleph-Tav theme of everything".

This of course is exactly what is occurring in the Merkabah meditation when we place our Aleph, which is our sense of Unity, at the center of the Tav, which is our inner Cross of Construction representing the cross of space-time. The intersecting lines of this, as you may remember, are the Heart Center. It should be remembered that the Hebrew "Aleph-Tav" is the same as the Greek "Alpha-Omega".

This same type of scenario also occurs earlier in the text in chapter I, verse 13. Here we find YHVH sealing the six directions of 3 dimensional space with different combinations of the 3 letters (YHV) that make up the name;

> "Turned towards the upper, sealed it with YHV. Six: sealed the lower, turned towards the underneath & sealed it with YVH. Seven: sealed the East-with HYV. Eight: sealed the West-with HVY. Nine: sealed the South-with VYH. Ten: sealed the North-with VHY".

**Y**, Yod =1O, is the projection of Aleph in to the temporal world. **H**, Hay = 5, is the archetype of universal life. **V**, Vav or Waw = 6, is the fertilizing agent, that which impregnates or activates.

It appears again near the end of the text in chapter V, verse 1. This time in an astrological context that, when the directions are followed, gives us a perfect diamond shape. The points of the diamond are represented by 7 planets, six outer one inner. *Shabatai* (Saturn), is at the top, with *Tsedeq* (Jupiter) below, *Meadim* (Mars) in the East, *Hhamah* (The Sun) in the West, *Nogah* (Venus) in the North, *Kawkab* (Mercury) in the South, and *Lvanah* (The Moon) inside at the center. With precise details as to their placement, each line represents one of the signs of the zodiac, and its correspondence to certain letters of the Hebrew alphabet:

| | | | | |
|---|---|---|---|---|
| East-North: | "Toleh" | = | (Aries) | Hay |
| East-South: | "Shaur" | = | (Taurus) | Waw |
| East-High: | "Theomim" | = | (Gemini) | Zayn |
| East-Low: | "Sartann" | = | (Cancer) | Hhayt |
| North-High: | "Arieh" | = | (Leo) | Tayt |
| North-Low: | "Betolah" | = | (Virgo) | Yod |
| West-South: | "Moznaim" | = | (Libra) | Lammed |
| West-North: | "Aaqrav" | = | (Scorpio) | Noun |
| West-High: | "Qaschoth" | = | (Sagittarius) | Sammekh |
| West-Low: | "Guedi" | = | (Capricorn) | Ayn |
| South-High: | "Deli" | = | (Aquarius) | Tsadde |
| South-Low: | "Daghirn" | = | (Pisces) | Qof |

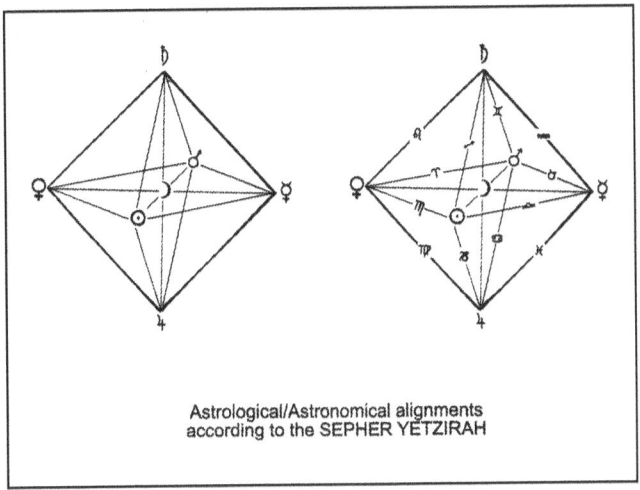

Astrological/Astronomical alignments
according to the SEPHER YETZIRAH

If we follow these directions for our selves and avoid the watch dog-ma, we can plainly see the shape that is being relayed to us.

---

[16] Sepher Yetzirah, Gra, Warsaw, 1884

# THE DIAMOND AND THE
# UNIFIED FIELD

ow that we've established that this shape is found in these ancient rituals and texts, we should look at its deeper meaning. This will be easier for us to do if we first look at the **Sepher Yetzirah**, from which we took 3 of our examples. A quote from Carlo Suares [17] regarding the significance of this text, points us in the right direction:

> "It is a great mistake to think that The Sepher Yetzirah is a book that can be understood after reading it once. Those most qualified - not to read, but study it - are physicists engaged in advanced scientific research. By showing that the energizing properties of the Autiot (Hebrew letter/numbers) have a dual cosmic flow, the way to an essential stage of modern physics is cleared: mainly, the study of consciousness in its material manifestations, as energy."

Carlo, through his 40 years of work with the ancient Hebrew texts, came to realize that the Hebrew alphabet was a highly sophisticated, self-embedded language based in physics. This brings us to our next stop - **the world of physics**.

To understand why this shape is so important we have to first look at what the diamond (Octahedron) represents. It's here that we find ourselves in the world of physics, or more specifically, quantum physics and the unified field.

Here's how it works: the Unified Field Universe has only one substance, which is consciousness. That substance is viewed as a sort of vast ocean of undifferentiated energy, a kind of cosmic soup or jelly. The only self-organizing shape that is able to keep its form is a donut shaped vortex called a "Torus". It is the only shape that can, by feeding back on itself (turning itself inside out), self stand as a wave form. This is basically what a smoke ring does. From the standpoint of physics, the universe arranges itself as Toruses (donuts) which are actually 3 dimensional sine waves. These 3D sine waves directly correlate to the 3-axis spin of the Octahedron, which is actually a geometrical representation of a Torus.

There's a whole lot more stuff involved here that we're not really going to get into. Stuff that has to do with symmetry, and things called heterodynes that relate to the addition and multiplication of wave lengths, and the way that they are able to meet or nest without interfering with each other. The point is that the Octahedron represents the universal archetype of cosmic intelligent motion, and it more or less explains how the vibratory nature of the Cosmic Intelligence **_conspires_** with the raw substance of Light to get it to enfold on itself, to become what we call *Matter*. Basically, it represents the source of all things, seen and unseen. (Don't worry if you don't understand the technical stuff, it's only here to make a point.)

The initiates of some of the ancient mystery schools knew all this very well. It was one of the secrets that they kept safely guarded. We all know one of the best ways to keep something secret is to hide it in plain sight, which is where at least part of it seems to have been the whole time.

---

[17] Carlo Suares, The Qabala Trilogy, Pg. 417, Shambhalah Publications, 1985

CONSPIRACY OF LIGHT

# Quantum Meta-Physics

We are going to delve a bit further into the realm of the physicist. Quantum physicists are for the most part, a group of biologists and mathematicians who act as sort of modern day philosophers. They use theoretical mathematics and other developmental processes as their medium of expression. An interesting thing began to occur quite a few years ago in the field of science referred to as quantum physics, specifically in the area known as quantum mechanics.

Basically, quantum mechanics is a type of mathematical system that deals with the potential behavior of the particles that go into the construction of what is commonly referred to as reality, or physical matter. All the possible information concerning any given particle or object is referred to as the object's 'wave function.' The wave function itself refers to the probable or predictable behavior of the object. The intended purpose of quantum mechanics has been to develop a mathematical system through which you could predict the probable behavior or motion of a given number of objects within a given field. In other words, how the objects would interact with each other - simple, right?

Now, the system as it stood worked very well if you didn't intend to actually measure and observe the process that you were constructing the equation for. However, it soon became apparent that if you did intend to observe and measure the process, you had to add into your equation the fact that you were doing

Application of Ancient Physics                    97

so, because it and you had now become an integral part of the field structure.   Not only that, it soon became quite obvious that the scientists themselves were constructed of the very same particles they were trying to observe.   This in turn lead some to the realization that the universe itself was a system that was designed to be aware of itself, because they found that they simply couldn't separate themselves from what they were observing.   This is where the proverbial *Shift* hits the fan.

Basically, what happens when you factor in the element of conscious observance into the construction of a quantum mechanical equation is that the quantum mechanistic motion ceases to be wholly predictable.    In fact, in the words of one physicist:

> "It becomes grossly non-linear when conscious beings enter the picture and for the most part, the wave function ceases to be wholly recognizable as a wave function". [18]

The simplest way out of this difficulty was to accept the conclusion that the joint system of conscious being plus object cannot be described by a wave function after the interaction.  To most this seemed to be more of a convenient avoidance of the issue, than an actual answer.

Getting back to the point, the mathematical equations seemed to point out a simple fact that has been known by mystics and initiates of the ancient mystery schools from the beginning.   Simply, that consciousness effects the nature of what is perceived to be reality, as well as the particle motion of matter.

For some of the more classical physicists this new perspective of how consciousness affects reality was viewed as unacceptable, and for the most part ignored. For others, it opened up new ways of looking at the nature of reality, and gave them avenues of understanding and explaining some of the more mysterious processes that are involved in the formation of life and the Universe.

At Princeton, David Bohm taught a course on the "Philosophy of Quantum Mechanics - The Universe as a Field of Thought". Einstein, also teaching his theory of relativity there at the time, was thought to hold an opposing point of view, though in truth the two became fast friends. Later, this type of view was to lead Dr. John Hagelin to win the Nobel Prize in physics for his "Flipped S.U.5" or Super Unified Field theory. Eventually, this allowed developmental biologists such as Rupert Sheldrake to develop a very good explanation for the complex arrangement of atoms, molecules, crystals, cells, tissues, organs, organisms, and societies of organisms.

In order to understand what this all means, we have to first look at the role of genes in the DNA structure. The genetic code in the DNA molecules determines the sequence of amino acids in proteins. It does not, however, specify the way the proteins are arranged in the cells, the way the cells are arranged in the tissues, the arrangement of tissues in organs, and the organs in organisms. This has lead a number of developmental biologists to suggest that the concept of genetic programs is highly misleading, and therefore should ultimately be abandoned.

Genetic programs are usually viewed as being something like computer programs, only computer programs are designed by intelligent beings and genetic programs are supposed to have been thrown together by chance. This has lead Sheldrake [19] to remark:

> "Given the right genes and hence the right proteins, and the right systems by which protein synthesis is controlled, the organism is somehow supposed to assemble itself automatically. This is rather like delivering the right materials to a building site at the right times and expecting a house to grow spontaneously."

This has lead Sheldrake to postulate the existence of something he calls *morphic fields*, which contain an inherent memory function. He further suggests that there is a continuous spectrum of these fields, which include morphogenetic fields, behavioral fields, mental fields, and social and *cultural fields*. The way these fields work goes something like this: All natural systems inherit the collective memory from all previous things of their kind through a process called *morphic resonance*. The result is that the patterns of development and behavior become increasingly habitual through repetition, and therefore become a kind of programmed blue print for further development.

This sounds very much like what H. P. Blavatsky and others refer to as the *ethers*, in which are contained the blue prints of life. To get a better picture of how this works, imagine that there is a large series of inter-connecting energy fields around everything. These function as a recording device that is able to record all data concerning the motion, behavior, and organization of all forms of energy (*matter is itself, a form of energy*) down to the most infinitesimally small particle. These energy fields store the information and then transmit the data to all newly emerging, reforming substances, giving them instructions on how to behave based on the previous behavior of all the substances of the same form. Hans Jenny speaks of such organizing fields as being of a rhythmic vibratory nature. He refers to this process as "*periodicity*" because of its periodically recurring nature.

"How extensively the triadic nature of vibration is found, is brought home to us when we realize that the complex organizations of movement, of rhythmic Systems (circulation and respiration), and of nerve physiology become evident to us as frequencies and modulations including amplitude modulations.

"The dominant role of the periodic in other organs and their functions is merely mentioned in passing. (Protein synthesis, the model of genetic information in the living cell, respiratory enzyme chains, catalysis, etc.). He (mankind) lives in these fields, in that he grasps them and acts with them, in them, on them, through them, and only thus takes on a tangible appearance himself." [20]

[18] Quantum Theory and Measurement, Princeton University textbook, 1976
[19] Rupert Sheldrake, A New Science of Life, Paladin Books, 1983
[20] Hans Jenny, Kymatik, Pg. 181-182, Basilius Presse Basel

# THE MATTER OF MATTER

The main purpose of what is nowadays called particle physics has been to find out just what exactly lies at the heart of physical matter at the atomic level. The classical Newtonian view was that everything was made up of hard indestructible atoms that were actually minute separate physical particles. These particles were thought to act very much the same as moving billiard balls, constantly colliding and bouncing off of each other, none the worse for wear. The movement of the atomic structure was believed to be a purely mechanical process. The idea was that the Universe was made up of separate physical atoms that some how got together to form larger physical objects that were themselves separate from the space around them, and that everything existed in a separate field of time. This was not only the Western scientific view before the 20th century, it was - and for the most part still is - the way the Western world lives and views life itself. It wasn't until the development of 20th century technology in the form of particle accelerators, and bubble chambers that the classical Newtonian view of the atomic world could, and would finally be laid to rest.

The first experiments using a particle accelerator - in an attempt to view the sub-microscopic atomic world - showed some very interesting, albeit unexpected results. The idea behind these experiments was to see whether the basic constituents of matter were indestructible and unchangeable, or whether they were composite objects that could be broken up time and again until you finally arrived at a basic, smallest, indivisible particle. The answer to the question turned out to be both yes and no. Yes you can break the particles up, and no you can't break them into smaller pieces. What happens when you slam these particles together, is that they break into more particles of the exact same size. In other words, you create more particles. Further study showed that what was once perceived to actually be minute, solid particles, really have no solidity, at least not in the classical sense.

The structure of an atom is composed almost entirely of empty space. The nucleus of an atom is about one hundred thousand times smaller than the atom itself. The main elements that make up the structure of an atom, are actually points of energy whirling at various rates of speed: *600 miles per second for electrons and 40,000 miles per second for the nucleons* (i.e. protons & neutrons,) though in truth nothing is actually whirling or spinning. What they do have is angular momentum, sort of like a top, but no actual spin.

So, in much the same way that a propeller spinning at a very high rate of speed can sometimes look like a solid disk, the atomic structure itself can present itself as seemingly solid forms, that basically... really aren't. In other words, solidity is entirely dependent on the point of view. As the old saying goes, *things may really not be as they seem.*

Another interesting fact was that you couldn't get an accurate understanding of these particles if you tried to view them as separate entities. This is due to the fact that they're actually constantly moving, changing assemblies of energy within an overall universal process or cosmic web. As physicist Fritjof Capra puts it:

"In the New World view, the universe is seen as a dynamic web of interrelated events. None of the properties of any part of this web is (more) fundamental (than any other part), they all follow from the properties of the other parts, and the overall consistency of their mutual interrelations determines the structure of the entire web." [21]

Speaking further of *S-matrix* theory, also called the *bootstrap hypothesis* - a synthesis of quantum, field, and relativity theories - Capra states:

"The bootstrap hypothesis not only denies the fundamental constituents of matter, but accepts no fundamental entities whatsoever - no fundamental laws, equations or principles - and thus abandons another idea which has been an essential part of natural science for hundreds of years". [21]

---

[21] F. Capra, The Tao of Physics, Pg. 286, Shambala Publications, 1975

# ACADEMY OF UR

# POST-GRADUATE:

# KINDERVERSITY

# OBSERVATIONS

From a certain point of view, the objective of the consciousness as it relates to the Earth experience seems to be one of being a fully functioning, unifying force or presence. If we are lead to understand that the consciousness exerts a directional force on the particle processes that make up matter in its undifferentiated form, then the role of the consciousness may be to bring order out of chaos. On the other hand, the role of consciousness may be, to simply participate in the game of existence/non-existence as a conscious focal point within an already perfect, well-ordered system. The possible implications of these statements are, to say the least, quite staggering either way you look at it.

What seems to be the most efficient method of investigating the workings of this process is to simply merge or unify the sense of self with the whole. From that standpoint all possibilities are included and there's no attachment to a particular point of view. The view of things as they actually are becomes abundantly clear.

There seem to be pit falls along the more linear paths of investigation. This occurs when the overall view is left behind completely, and a more minute focus is used in the investigation process. What happens here is that we get a bit-ified, or partial view of the process that is, as mentioned before, very Newtonian. This is the action-reaction method of observation. We basically observe that which we perceive to be an object - say a particle - has action. We soon realize that the observed action was actually a reaction to the action of something else. From this we see that that action too was a reaction and so on down the line. Needless to say, this method of observation can be quite lengthy, and never really seems to give us a view of precisely what's going on. When we hold an expanded view, we are able to see the overall motion of the whole. From this standpoint, we soon realize that we are observing events, relations, operations, and forms rather than things and substances. We are then able to go back and examine the minute details as they relate to the process as a whole, and thus develop even greater understanding. To use a quote from the 12th century Qabalistic text called the *Sepher ha-Bahir:*

**From above to below we know. But from below to above we do not.**

This line of information has been presented here is to point out two things. First, that modern science and metaphysics are both aware that this process exists as the functioning of the Universe. Secondly, certain very important experiential aspects of this function that pertain to you and mankind as a whole are COMPLETELY RE-PROGRAMMABLE!!! This is the reason that all of the information in this text, and many others like it both ancient and new, is being presented again at this time. We are all being given the chance to change not only the direction of the currently agreed upon level of reality, but actually change the very structural foundations of what is perceived to be reality itself.

# RE-PROGRAMMING THE LOCAL CONTINUUM

**Y**ou're constantly doing it. We're doing it right 'Now'. It's a moment by moment process. Every word, every action, every thought effects everything around us, to a much greater degree than some of us may realize. The course of our future reality is created by everything we do in the 'Now'. When enough of us understand the message that stands behind the Merkabah, and the "Mitakuye Oyasin" of the Native Americans, (Lakota saying meaning: We are all related), and truly begin to act in accordance with that message, we will be able to collectively effect the resonant structure of the morphic fields to such an extent that everyone who wants to, will wake up. This is what Sheldrake calls the 100th monkey effect. That's all there is to it, and it only takes "one" to get the ball rolling. Look at what **Guatama** (the Buddha) and **Yhshwh** (Jesus), as well as many others have been able to do. No matter what we've been told about them, the simple fact is that they were Human beings, Just the same as you or I. This is what Yhshwh was trying to tell us when he reportedly said, "*You shall do even greater things than I.*" Well, he's right, you will...

Looking at this from the technical point of view, the blue print of the behavior of things is programmed directly into the morphic fields by constant repetitive action, the more repetitive the action, the stronger the program becomes. When we break the pattern of motion, we are in essence working directly with the behavioral blue print. If say, for instance, we have somehow developed a stressful or fearful behavioral pattern, we can re-program the pattern by the repetitive practice of calm behavior. This not only makes us more comfortable, it makes everyone and everything we come into contact with more comfortable, which in turn helps them to re-program the field themselves. This may seem very basic but it actually has far greater implications once we understand that the thing that we call reality takes its direction at the behest of the consciousness, and not the other way around. The idea here is to go directly to the source of things and work with the blue print itself. As any good architect will tell you the most efficient way of changing the construction of anything is to first change the blue print.

To bring this back to a more basic level, if we observe a pattern of behavior in other members of our cosmic family that seems to be somehow detrimental, the most direct method of dealing with those patterns is to simply not do them ourselves. A lot of information is beginning to be presented to all of us now, in many forms, on the technical aspects of how this all works. The point of which is to show that _it does work._ (If you look at the first Super-Luminal motion that takes place in the pre-matter state, you will understand this.)

The Great thing is that we don't need to understand all of this in order to make it work, all we have to do is keep an open Heart and an open Mind, the rest will come when we're ready. Just be patient. One more thing, there's nothing to be worried about because everyone gets through this one way or another.

# The Universe as a Field of Consciousness

As should be quite obvious by now, the information here is based entirely upon the point of view that the universe as a whole is a single, self-expressive, conscious, organic, living, breathing entity. And, that all motion, form, and substance, including what you think of as yourself, are merely ways in which that entity expresses itself. This statement is by no means as outrageous as it may seem to some. Its greatest supporters, as mentioned before, can be found among the ranks of modern physicists and spiritual mystics alike. As a general warning it should probably be pointed out that some of the information in this section may push the buttons of some of us whose sense of identity is firmly wrapped up in what we do - as opposed to what and who we are.

What will be addressed here are some of the more subtle dynamics of consciousness as it relates to the mystical experience of what we call everyday life. Although, having used the word mystical, the realization comes that the general interpretation of the word tends to present a type of view that is all together, other worldly. Strictly speaking, this isn't exactly what is meant. What is being alluded to by the use of the word mystical is an experience of the world, not as a series of separate, unrelated things, but as a single process or pattern in which the *things* of the world are seen as interrelated forms within an over all pattern. In more basic terms, this is the experience of everyday life as relationship.

This type of experience is quite often referred to as a spiritual or mystical experience, in which we suddenly seem to lose all sense of being separate from our surroundings. The sense of self and other disappears, and we have an experience of total oneness with the entire universe. In the history of Judeo Christian thinking this has often been referred to as having an experience of the Divine. The point of view being that, the everyday world as it exists in the ever present 'Now', is absolutely and gloriously perfect in its seeming state of imperfection. From this perspective, all opposites become mere aspects of an overall unitary motion of cosmic proportions. Further more, along with this comes the realization that absolutely nothing needs to be done about making any of it better, and that there is really no one who needs to be saved from anything.

Some may perceive this an altogether dangerous statement, if not a lazy one. It may, in fact, seem to some to be an invitation to anarchy. This could not be farther from the truth. The point being that someone who has had this type of experience has such an all encompassing view of the universe as being an aspect of themselves, that it would never occur to them to act in a fashion that could possibly harm anyone or anything. This includes interfering with another's life course. From what is considered the highest point of view, there is only One Being/Non-Being here, and what you experience as everyday life, is the way in which that Being/Non-Being has chosen to learn about itself.

To use Zen terminology, this experience is called *Satori* or enlightenment. It is this type of experience that many of us, who have sometimes viewed ourselves as "new age" thinkers, seem to be trying to attain and at the same time, are avoiding like the plague. This phenomenon is by no means unique to new agers. It is an inherent predicament that all of us, who might from time to time, think of ourselves as more *spiritually* advanced or gifted than someone else, can find ourselves in. The very existence of this phenomena itself could quite easily be missed due to the subtle nature of the dynamics that are involved.

What seems to happen is that a general universal message of love and acceptance is used as a basic corner stone upon which all the numerous teachings channeled or otherwise, are founded. The predicament lies, not in the message, but in the way the information is related to. In order to explain this more easily, the use of a Buddhist analogy might be helpful. An Ancient Buddhist saying states, "*If in your travels, you should meet the Buddha on the road, kill him.*" In other words, if at any point we should see ourselves as being separate from anything whatsoever, kill the thought or perception immediately. The idea being, that the path of liberation and enlightenment is one of absolute and total unity. The aim is to have this, not so much as an intellectual concept, but as a total sensual experience, though at first we may have to be satisfied with the intellectual aspect alone.

The dynamics of the situation are those that are tied to the sense of self. In the case of channeled information, the dynamics are, *who or what is the source of the information, and what and who is it that is receiving said information.* If the point of transmission is viewed as more special, or better than, or separate from the point of reception, we may be missing the subtle point that the nature of the universe is one of total unity. At the same time, if the point of reception views itself as more special, or better than, or separate from its fellow beings and surroundings because of its ability to receive such messages, the same subtle dynamics come into play. In the words of Ray Stanford, who is himself a channel:

> "The currently popular phenomenon of channeling, while supposedly affirming potential of inner power, is alleged in seeming philosophical contradiction, to come almost invariably from some outside entity. If the professed, personal inner power is so wonderful to the channels and their followers, one might wonder just why they are mere conduits (channels) instead of sources, and whether their alleged teachers have really developed their own inner spiritual resources." [22]

This is by no means meant to be an attack on channeling, it is only meant to point out some things that we might want to look at.

Next we come to a question pertaining to the information itself, namely - if the information is perceived to be valid from our point of view, how is the information utilized? First off, the validity of any line of information is dependent entirely upon one's particular point of view. A limited and restrictive line of information is perfectly valid for one whose general outlook, is itself, limited and restrictive. The same holds true for the one whose outlook is more expansive and less limited. From a unified perspective, both are equally valid and both are equally liberating. This particular point of view however, is itself, no more or less valid than any other. The only difference may be that it knows that it is no more or less so.

As far as the use of the information is concerned, not using pertinent information is sort of like buying an ax, putting it next to a wood pile, and expecting the wood to somehow chop itself. In other words, how is the information being applied in our experience of everyday life, and more to the point; *is it* actually being applied, and not just shared? Remember that the application of any tool is the only true measure of its usefulness.

Next we will take a look at the *intermediate realms of power* in which exist magical and psychic abilities of all types. While these abilities can be wonderful and invaluable tools of liberation, they never the less can also become traps due to their easy use in the game of *spiritual one-up-manship*. This plays into the predicament that is presented by the subtle dynamics mentioned earlier.

Now, as wonderful as we may find these abilities to be, they are not necessarily indicative of one's state of liberation. Here once again, we will use a Buddhist analogy:

It seems that among his many students, the Buddha had two in particular that were very gifted. Of the two, one was thought to be a great and wonderful sage by the people of the nearby villages, because of his ability to manifest things out of thin air. The other, while totally liberated, was never the less viewed as being quite ordinary by the people because he exhibited no special abilities. The Buddha, being quite aware of the situation, one day called the students together and asked the student with the special abilities to manifest a tiger. The student responded to the request by immediately making a tiger appear before them, where upon, the tiger turned toward the student who had brought it forth and began to growl and advance towards him. The student, upon seeing this, immediately became frightened and ran away. The Buddha responded to the student's apparent lack of understanding toward the nature of his own created illusion by explaining; as you can see, he is afraid of his own creation, and therefore not truly liberated.

The application of this analogy by the Buddha metaphorically points out the general predicament that most of mankind seems to find itself in; specifically, that of being an integral part of the process of creation, and being afraid of it at the same time.

It should be pointed out that having these powers by no means negates the possibility of becoming liberated. There are many Tibetan monks who are totally liberated, and yet are quite capable of performing these types of things. One of the reasons that we don't see both of these aspects together that often, is that the path through the *intermediate realms of power* has a tendency to make one feel special, and therefore presents a sense of separation.

Conversely, the path of pure liberation presents one with such an overwhelming sense of total unity and well-being, and a view of the perfection of things as they are, that one could really give a care about such matters. When and if these things are ever done from a state of pure liberation, they are usually done purely out of a sense of play, and for no other reason than that. This is simply because the ones who *know*, know there is nothing to be attained, and absolutely nothing to be gained by such actions. Basically speaking, you're all it, it's all you, and it's all perfect. So, why mess with things?

As a very wise being once said:

> "If you think you're here to make the world a better place, you're missing the point."

As for anything that's been written here, please don't take anyone's word about any of this. *Go check things out for yourself.* That's the only way we're ever really able to find out what truth is. None of this is intended to convert anyone over to another point of view or change anyone's thinking, because actually, whatever we seem to be doing or thinking is absolutely perfect the way it is. This is all done purely out of a sense of play and delight in the way that the universe moves in and of itself. The information presented here merely brings to Light some things that we may want to look at as we play the game of spiritual liberation. Truth be known, none of this is ultimately important.

---

[22] Fatima Prophecy, Ray Stanford, Pg. 85, Ballantine Books, 1991

# The Legend of the Fall That Wasn't

## Another Way of Looking at an Old Fairy Tale

 ong, long ago, in a Galaxy far, far away there was... sorry, wrong story...

In The Beginning... (well, shortly thereafter at any rate) things were very much the same as they are now (in the higher octaves anyway). You know, a lot of unlimited love, light and freedom. In fact, for the most part, that's all there was, lots and lots of unlimited limitlessness. Oh yeah, and a whole bunch of Heavy Duty Light Beings. (Or was that Light Duty Heavy Beings?) Anyway, everything at that point was possible, all the raw material to make anything you could think of was right on hand in unlimited supply. That's about all you had to do to make something. Just think of it, and there it was! You could do anything, anything at all. Everything was possible. (And still is, as a matter of fact.)

Now one of the favorite things to do at that point was to create new realms, or worlds of experience, sort of like holographic virtual reality games of immense proportions, and then get lost in them. One of the things that these beings really appreciated was difference. They loved it. (Along with everything else.) They couldn't get enough of it - the more difference, the better. You see to them difference was variety and variety, as the saying goes, is the spice of life. That's the reason they created those virtual reality worlds. They were different.

The way these sorts of games or worlds were created was really interesting. They usually started out as a sort of brain storming session that could involve any number of beings. First they would figure out what they wanted to do, then they would figure out how they wanted it to work. Then they would just sit around and visually concentrate whatever it was that they wanted, into being. If their creation turned out to be a particularly good one, they would invite everyone in to check it out. When they decided that they were through with it, all they had to do was stop thinking about it, and it would disappear. If they wanted to keep it around, however, that was a different story.

Small things were really quite easy to do. However, the larger, more complex projects required much more effort. You see, in order to make something that wouldn't dissipate when you took your focus off it, you had to first design it so that it could pretty much function on its own with a minimum amount of maintenance. This required some sort of Eco-system. Secondly, you had to keep your focus on it for a long period. The longer it was held in focus, the denser it became. Long periods didn't really matter to these beings because they were eternal - they didn't die. They had special areas where they could create these projects that were going to be around for awhile, usually away from the more densely populated dimensional levels of the universe. These areas became known as "experimental zones". (The key syllable here is "mental".) The really interesting thing about these projects was that not only were they entertaining, they were educational as well.

They were basically centers of conscious evolution, you know, a place where the Universe taught itself about itself, a University.

The way these things worked went something like this. The group of beings who came up with the idea for a particular zone would hold the structural form in place, while another group of beings projected themselves into the structure. Their task was to check things out to make sure that the zone could become self-operational/sustainable. If it looked like it could, the next thing that they did was to set up the curriculum in such a way that it would naturally follow a sequential path of development, which could be periodically adjusted if the need should arise. Next, they went around and hid clues about what was going on that either wouldn't be found or, if found, wouldn't be understood until a certain point in the curriculum had been reached. Then they simply wiped out the memory grid, and went to school. This allowed the first group to take their attention off of the project, as the ones who projected in were now holding the structure in place. The first group could then begin working as administrative advisors to the project. You see the wiping out of the memory grid completely focused their attention on the structure itself because they didn't remember that anything else existed. And that alone was more than enough to keep the structure intact. Pretty ingenious, huh?

In the meanwhile, the ones who had projected in now had no clue what was going on at all. They felt lost and alone, not realizing that they had helped set the whole thing up, and that the whole object of the place was to learn your way out of it and help others that were interested do the same. The curriculum itself was specifically designed to operate in conjunction with the cyclic motion of the structure itself. Each time the structure reached a certain point in a cycle, the curriculum would go to the next phase. More would be learned, and some of the memory would return. Eventually, the curriculum would be completed, and full memory would be restored. The structure itself would then become a fully self-sustaining playground, and a place of higher learning that would assist in the development of further projects. Best of all: Everyone graduates, one way or another, and They All Live Happily Ever After... THE BEGINNING. (What? Did you think there was an end to this story?) Remember the hide and seek game that was mentioned earlier in the book? Well... Tag! You're it...!

# *WELCOME TO THE CROWN OF CREATION*

# SUMMARY

We are all part of a single Triadic system of cosmic creation. Strictly speaking, regardless of what we've been told, the simple fact is that everything is Sacred, everything is Holy, and everything and everyone is equally Divine. The operation of the universe is not based on some sort of a medieval monarchical hierarchy in which we need to earn 'Spiritual Brownie points' in order to progress through. It is a dynamic self-expressive Holarchy. The existence of any one thing is solely dependent on the existence of everything else, and visa versa.

The worlds of Light and darkness, and spirit and matter, are in truth made up of a single energetic vibratory substance called Consciousness. We in essence are conscious focal points of a Self Aware Universe, and to put it as simply as possible, "We and everything else are ONE" and there's really nothing we can or need to do about it. Just relax, open up to it, Love it all, and what ever you choose to do, have fun doing it…

# SUGGESTED READING AND OTHER SOURCES

A New Science of Life, Rupert Sheldrake, Paladin Books, 1983

Book of Knowledge; The Keys of Enoch, by J. Hurtak, 1973

Godwin's Cabalistic Encyclopedia, Llewellyn Publications, 1994

Isis Unveiled & The Secret Doctrine, by H. P. Blavatsky, Theosophical University Press.

Kymatic, by Hans Jenny, Basilius Presse, A. G. Basel, Printed in Switzerland

Naka Wicape Wicoha: Universal & Spiritual Laws by Standing Elk, and Friends

Psychology and Religion: East and West, C.G. Jung, CW II, 1953-78

Stalking the Wild Pendulum, Itzhak Bentov, Destiny Books

Stan Tenen's work at the Meru Foundation, web site http://www.meru.org/

The Lazy Mans Guide to Enlightenment; by Thadeus Golas

The Qabala Trilogy, by Carlo Suares, Shambhala Books

The Science of Enlightenment; a tape series by Shinzen Young, Sounds True Audio, 735 Walnut street, Boulder, CO, 80302

The Self Aware Universe, by Professor Amit Goswami, Ph.D.

The Tao of Physics, by Fritjof Capra, Shambhala Books

The Way of Zen, or anything else written by Alan Watts

Theon of Smyrna, Wizards Bookshelf, Publisher

Top Sacred, Third Eye Only; work shop, Chelsea Flor

# THE MOST IMPORTANT
# SOURCE OF INFORMATION IS...

# YOU!

# BIBLIOGRAPHY

1. Godwin's Cabalistic Encyclopedia, pg. 38, Llewellyn Publications, 1994

2. Webster's Unabridged College Dictionary, 1984

3. Theon of Smyrna, Wizards Bookshelf, Publisher

4. The Women's Encyclopedia of Myths and Secrets, Castle Books edition, by Barbara G. Walker has some really good information on the subject.

5. C.G. Jung, Psychology and Religion: West and East, CW II, 1953-78

6. Klymatik by Hans Jenny, Basilius Presse Basel

7. The Secret Doctrine, H.P. Blavatsky, Theosophical University Press

8. Stalking the Wild Pendulum, Itzhak Bentov, Pg. 23-25, Destiny Books, Publisher, 1977

9. NIDA Research Monograph Series 146 * Hallucinogens: An Update, Pg. 92-116, 1994

10. National Institute of Allergy and Infectious Diseases, national Institutes of Health, News Release, Sept. 23, 1998

11. Excerpt from a private letter to H.P. Blavatsky from one of the beings she refers to as the "Mahatmas".

12. J. Hurtak, Book of Knowledge-the Keys of Enoch, 1973

13. Excerpt from personal conversations with Chelsea Flor.

14. Sefer Yetzirah, Gra Version, Warsaw, 1884 Edition

15. J. Hurtak, Book of Knowledge; The Keys of Enoch, 1973

16. Sepher Yetzirah, Gra, Warsaw, 1884

17. Carlo Suares, The Qabala Trilogy, Pg. 417, Shambhalah Publications, 1985

18. Quantum Theory and Measurement, Princeton University textbook, 1976

19. Rupert Sheldrake, A New Science of Life, Paladin Books, 1983

20. Hans Jenny, Kymatik, Pg. 181-182, Basilius Presse Basel

21. F. Capra, The Tao of Physics, Pg. 286, Shambala Publications, 1975

22. Fatima Prophecy, Ray Stanford, Pg. 85, Ballantine Books, 1991

www.ingramcontent.com/pod-product-compliance
Lightning Source LLC
Chambersburg PA
CBHW031207260626
47169CB00004B/1282